Heirs to an Empire

Succession, Secrets and Scandal

Following the death of their father, English aristocrat Cedric Pemberton, it's time for the Pemberton heirs to stake their claim in the family empire.

From fashion and cosmetics to jewelry and fragrance, Aurora Inc. is a multinational company, with headquarters all over the world.

As the siblings take the lead in different divisions of the business, they'll face challenges, uncover secrets and learn to start listening to their hearts...

Gabi and Will's Story
Scandal and the Runaway Bride

Charlotte and Jacob's Story
The Heiress's Pregnancy Surprise

Arabella and Burke's Story
Wedding Reunion with the Best Man

Christophe and Sophie's Story
Mistletoe Kiss with the Millionaire

Anemone and Phillippe's Story
A Proposal in Provence

And finally,

Esme and Stephen's Story
The Heir's Cinderella Bride

Available now!

Dear Reader,

Here we are, the sixth and final book in the Heirs to an Empire series. I've loved writing these stories; I adore writing about big families with a few skeletons in the closet. When the series opened, Stephen Pemberton, the Earl of Chatsworth, was left at the altar, and throughout the series he hasn't always been the kindest person. But he's had his good moments, and when it came time to give him his happy-ever-after, I thought it was time you got to see that Stephen is actually just very human—dealing with a lot of pressure and holding on to his own hurts and disappointments.

Esme Flanagan is the only person to really see beneath that surface, because she knew Stephen as a child. They were best friends. And even though they live in entirely different worlds, sometimes it just takes a heart speaking to another heart to set things right. But not without some missteps, of course.

I hope you've enjoyed this series. Happy reading!

Donna

The Heir's Cinderella Bride

Donna Alward

Recycling programs
for this product may
not exist in your area.

ISBN-13: 978-1-335-73677-2

The Heir's Cinderella Bride

Copyright © 2022 by Donna Alward

For questions and comments about the quality of this book, please contact us at CustomerService@Harlequin.com.

Harlequin Enterprises ULC
22 Adelaide St. West, 41st Floor
Toronto, Ontario M5H 4E3, Canada
www.Harlequin.com

Printed in U.S.A.

Donna Alward lives on Canada's east coast with her family, which includes her husband, a couple of kids, a senior dog and two zany cats. Her heartwarming stories of love, hope and homecoming have been translated into several languages, hit bestseller lists and won awards, but her favorite thing is hearing from readers! When she's not writing, she enjoys reading (of course), knitting, gardening, cooking...and she is a *Masterpiece* addict. You can visit her on the web at donnaalward.com and join her mailing list at donnaalward.com/newsletter.

Books by Donna Alward

Harlequin Romance

Heirs to an Empire

Scandal and the Runaway Bride
The Heiress's Pregnancy Surprise
Wedding Reunion with the Best Man
Mistletoe Kiss with the Millionaire
A Proposal in Provence

South Shore Billionaires

Christmas Baby for the Billionaire
Beauty and the Brooding Billionaire
The Billionaire's Island Bride

Visit the Author Profile page
at Harlequin.com for more titles.

It might sound strange to dedicate a book to my deck, but I'm doing it. Dear deck, thank you for providing me with my "summer office." Sitting in the sunshine with my laptop, a cold drink and the sound of the birds are the best working conditions I could ask for.

Praise for
Donna Alward

"Ms. Alward wrote a beautiful love story that is not to be missed. She provided a tale rich with emotions, filled with sexual chemistry, wonderful dialogue, and endearing characters.... I highly recommend *Beauty and the Brooding Billionaire* to other readers."

—*Goodreads*

CHAPTER ONE

THERE WAS NOTHING worse for Stephen Pemberton, Earl of Chatsworth, than feeling as if he'd just been *handled*.

Not like he really stood a chance when his sisters and mother ganged up on him. And it wasn't as if his brother, William, or cousin, Christophe, had taken his side. They'd been conspicuously silent when Aurora had issued the edict that he was the one who must return to Chatsworth Manor to oversee the construction of the new garden, which was to be a memorial to his father, Cedric Pemberton, the late earl. Two weeks, his mother had said. Time to approve the plans and be there to oversee breaking ground and the initial installations. Oh, and there was the local gooseberry festival in the village. Wouldn't it be lovely to have a member of the family in attendance again?

No, it would not. Be lovely, that is. But he would go, because for years his father had gone and good-naturedly judged the contests for best preserves, pies and puddings made with the abundant fruit. And since Stephen was the current earl, he would carry on the tradition, paste on a smile, and then when the garden was well begun. Then he'd head back to Paris and his office at Aurora, Inc.'s headquarters where he was COO of the family empire of fashion, cosmetics, and jewelry.

The supervision of the memorial garden was nothing but a ruse. This was the family's way of "suggesting" he take a vacation. At first, he'd balked. But then Aurora had looked at him over the top of her Chanel reading glasses, and he'd reconsidered. Not for her sake, but for his.

Peace was in short supply within his family. For the past few years, he had been managing one crisis after another. Now that everyone was romantically paired up, it seemed all eyes were on him as the sole single sibling. And frankly, it was a relief to leave Paris and the meddling members of his family behind for a bit. Not that he would let them know that. They might think they'd "handled" him, but Stephen didn't do anything he didn't want to. He fully intended to spend the next several days in solitude, attending to Chatsworth estate business and avoiding whatever new drama the rest of the family cooked up.

Which was why he was now exiting the car in front of the manor house while the driver retrieved his bags.

Stephen let out a deep breath, and a measure of calm filled his body.

Home. Resentful, reluctant…whatever his feelings, he couldn't deny that out of all the family properties around the world, this was home to him. It always would be.

He shouldered one of the bags and the driver followed him up the cobbled walk to the massive oak door. Which remained firmly closed, instead of opening at his arrival.

He frowned. His appearance could hardly have gone unnoticed. With a sigh he lifted a hand, reaching for the knocker, then hesitated.

It was his own bloody house. Why did he have to knock?

Instead, he turned the heavy knob and opened it himself, stepping inside the foyer with his garment bag over his arm and tugging his suitcase along behind him as the driver departed.

He was greeted by heavy dark woodwork, polished floors, and unusual silence.

Where was everyone? And what exactly did the staff get up to when the family wasn't in residence? The last thing he wanted was to have a "conversation" with Mrs. Flanagan, the housekeeper. Something niggled at the edge of his brain. Mrs. Flanagan…she was ill, wasn't she? Maman had mentioned something about it when she'd given him the details about the festival and the landscape architect. Alarm skittered down his limbs. What if something had happened to Mrs. F? Was that why there was no sign of any staff?

Lord, he hoped not. Mrs. F had been the house-keeper at Chatsworth Manor ever since he was a boy. His fondest memories were of her, and of her daughter—

"Stephen?"

Stephen turned toward the sound and his eye-brows immediately lifted in surprise. The woman before him was definitely not the russet-haired housekeeper he'd known since he'd been a child. But she was familiar. She'd barely changed at all. "Esme?"

"Good afternoon, my lord."

She'd recovered somewhat, and he watched with fascination as she schooled her features into a polite mask and carefully modulated her voice. It annoyed him. There was only one other time she'd ever called him "my lord," and it was branded on his brain as if it had just happened yesterday, in-stead of when he was thirteen. It had been their one and only fight, and it had been a big one.

He let go of the handle of his suitcase. "What are you doing here?" Her eyebrows lifted just the tiniest bit, and his cheeks heated as he realized he'd sounded less than polite. "I mean, I wasn't expecting to see you."

"I'm overseeing the household."

Stephen stared at Esme. The last time he'd seen her, he'd been barely a teenager and she'd been all of twelve. Her mother, Mrs. Flanagan, had been the housekeeper here since he'd turned four. She'd had a three-year-old daughter who had become his best playmate. Esme, with her dancing green eyes and red hair and sense of adventure.

But more than twenty years had passed. He'd gone away to school. She'd gone on to…what? He was ashamed to admit he didn't know. Regardless, she was far more subdued than that precocious child now, standing before him in black trousers and a black shirt, comfortable shoes on her feet. Even though years had passed, though, there was no mistaking her. Her coppery hair was pulled back in a utilitarian twist and her clothing was plain, but she was just as beautiful as he remembered, with soft, mossy green eyes and a dusting of freckles over her nose.

"Are you done staring, sir?"

He frowned. "First of all, don't call me sir. Or my lord. Or Lord Pemberton."

"Then what should I call you?" She stepped forward now, that implacable mask still in place. "You *are* Lord Pemberton. And I am a member of your staff."

She wasn't wrong, but the knowledge—and her uptight tone—grated. "I know it's been a while, but we've made mud pies together. Surely we're beyond that kind of formality."

She sighed, but her voice warmed slightly. "That was a long time ago."

His brows pulled together. "Where is everyone

else? Why is there no one at the door, or…" He looked around. "It's like you're the only one here."

She sighed again. "That's because I *am* the only one here. With no family in residence, nearly all the staff is on holidays."

"Except you, apparently."

"And the gardener, and the grooms at the stables. But I'm the only one in the house for the next ten days."

Which was damned inconvenient, since that was pretty much how long he would be here at Chatsworth. How could Maman have suggested a thing if she'd known? And she must have authorized it. The urge to rub his hand over his eyes was overwhelming. Hopefully it had just slipped Maman's mind, and she wasn't having her own crisis. Keeping his brothers and sisters in line was a full-time job, it seemed. Adding worry about Maman gave him a headache.

"Honestly, I feel the need to be more formal than I would normally be in order for the staff to take me seriously. I'm not my mother, you know?" She turned those lovely green eyes up to his and he was speechless for a moment.

The red-haired, impish girl had grown into an incredibly alluring woman.

"Speaking of, where is your mother? I wasn't aware she'd left. Did she retire?" He hoped his slight recollection about her health was wrong.

Esme shook her head. "No, she's been ill. Look,

why don't I get you some coffee, and I can give you the details in the library? Marjorie left a Victoria Sponge in the kitchen before she left yesterday."

It was a favorite, and his stomach growled. "I didn't have lunch, so a sandwich before sponge would be appreciated as well, if you don't mind."

"I'll see to it right away."

"Thank you, Esme."

She turned to walk away, and his mind raced back to how many times they'd gotten into mischief together as children, how she'd never cared a bit that he was in line for the title. An ache settled in his chest. It might as well be a century ago. He certainly didn't resemble that fun-loving boy any longer.

"Esme?"

She turned around with a questioning expression, as if wondering if there was something else he needed. It was so odd, thinking of her waiting on him. That he was essentially her…boss.

"It's awfully good to see you."

She smiled then, and it lit up the room. "It's good to see you, too, Stephen."

Then she turned to the right and disappeared through a doorway, leading to the downstairs and the kitchens.

He turned left toward the library. Esme as the housekeeper. But how ill was Mrs. Flanagan, and why had Esme been the one to take over for her?

And why hadn't anyone told him?

* * *

Esme put together a full tray for Stephen's lunch, the weight of it heavy in her hands as she went back up the steps from the kitchens and to the library. She hadn't known he was coming, and it left her feeling totally off balance. The family always let the staff know when someone was going to be in residence. Now here she was, the interim housekeeper, and all the staff on holidays precisely because no one from the family was supposed to be here.

She'd manage. There was no way she was going to call anyone back from a well-deserved break. Unless, of course, she was ordered to. She was staff, after all. Not like she could forget. Stephen was ensconced in the library while she was the one holding the tray.

The library was her favorite room in the house. Always had been, with its delightfully rich furniture in dark wood and brocade fabrics, a massive fireplace, and walls covered with books from antique and rare titles to recent bestsellers. There was even a smaller bookcase in a corner that housed children's titles, along with pint-sized chairs for wee ones to curl up in. She'd spent a number of afternoons in that corner after school, either doing the meagre bit of homework she'd brought home or reading one of the titles that the earl had allowed her to borrow whenever she wanted.

Cedric Pemberton had been a good man. Certainly, he had been good to her mother and herself, providing the single mum with a reliable job and allowing Esme to tag along with his other children.

Now they were all grown up, and there was no disputing the evidence of that fact as she entered the library and saw Stephen sitting at the large desk—Cedric's old desk. Heavens, he was handsome—all dark looks, chiseled jaw, and broad shoulders. He was in the news occasionally, so it wasn't like his appearance was a shock, necessarily. But seeing him in person…hearing his voice… it set off a flood of happy memories. She doubted he knew how much his friendship had meant to her as a child, or how much she'd missed him when he'd turned thirteen and suddenly wasn't around anymore. The Pembertons had done the proper thing and sent him off to school.

"Your lunch," she said, approaching the desk, biting off the "sir" that threatened to escape her lips.

"Oh, thank you." He looked up from his laptop and offered a small smile, which was so tight it actually seemed to pain him. He looked at the assortment, then up at her. "You should have brought a cup for yourself."

"This isn't the old days," she chided gently. "I'm staff."

"I meant so we could talk about what will be happening this week."

That was her put in her place, then.

"Besides," he added, "having a conversation with you hovering above me feels weird."

-Esme sighed. "I'm fine." She pulled up a nearby chair, so she was closer to the desk. "I suppose this does provide an opportunity for us to talk about what your needs are for the next few weeks while you are home. Do you expect anyone from the rest of the family to be joining you?"

He added sugar to his coffee—no cream, she noted for future reference—and stirred it. "Doubtful. Charlotte is in Richmond while Jacob is working an assignment in Turkey. Bella and Burke are just back from their honeymoon, and Sophie is still apparently trying to catch up on sleep since the baby was born." He shuddered. "Everyone is getting married and having babies. Next I expect Will and Gabi will be adding to the grandchild list."

Stephen reached for his napkin and sandwich.

"I take it you're not into marriage and babies."

"Not exactly." He took a bite of his sandwich.

"That must be interesting, considering you're the heir."

His dark eyes hardened, almost imperceptibly, but Esme caught the coolness and wondered what was behind it.

"With my siblings procreating, it does take

some of the pressure off." He dabbed his lips with his napkin and sent her a look that she could only describe as cynical. "After being burned twice, I'm content with my life as it is."

Ah, yes. The broken engagements. Once, three years ago, maybe four, if her memory served correctly, he'd been set to marry Bridget Enys but the engagement had been broken off only a few months before the wedding, though no one seemed to know why. The more recent event, and far more scandalous, was Gabriella Baresi leaving him at the altar...and then marrying his brother, William. It certainly looked like there were no hard feelings now, but her mum had told her that Stephen had been livid when Gabi had disappeared on the day of the wedding, and a bear to live with for months, storming around, barking orders. Looking at his imperious expression now, she didn't find it a stretch to imagine. It might be best to leave that topic alone.

"So," Stephen said, breaking into her thoughts, "what's going on with your mum? Is she very ill?"

Esme nodded, worry churning in her stomach. Sometimes she nearly forgot as she went about her work, but the anxiety was always there, waiting for her when she took a moment to pause. "Ill enough. She has breast cancer. She had surgery and then radiation, but now she's starting chemotherapy. She's found her recovery from surgery more difficult than she expected, as she developed a post-op chest infection." Esme swallowed around the lump that seemed to form in her throat every time she thought of her mother in hospital, hooked to IVs and drainage tubes, so pale and tired. "She was so worried about her job—"

"She shouldn't be." He frowned and tilted his head a little. "My mother must know all of this. Odd she didn't tell me." He put down his sandwich and met her gaze directly. "Please tell me we are giving Mrs. Flanagan paid sick leave."

She smiled, relaxing a little. "Oh, yes. Lady Pemberton has been wonderful that way. She offered to pay Mum's wages while she's sick so she won't have financial struggles."

"Good." He gave a satisfied nod and took another bite of the sandwich. She softened just a little, too. In many ways, the man before her now was a cold stranger, but he'd immediately shifted into making sure her mother was cared for. It made her glad to see there was a good man beneath the cool exterior.

"What I meant before was…well, Mum was worried about who would look after the house." She grinned before she could stop herself. "I think Chatsworth Manor is her other child."

He smiled back. "And that's where you came in."

Heavens, when he smiled his whole face changed, morphing into something familiar that sent a pang through her chest. She nodded, pushing the feeling away. "I cleared it with my boss and took a leave of absence from my job at the inn. Goodness knows I've spent enough time here, working odd jobs, helping Mum out from time to time. With the family not in residence, it's a small staff to oversee." A smile flirted with her lips. "And now they're on holiday for a week. Cushiest job I've ever had."

It wasn't a lie. She'd worked as a housemaid, as hotel housekeeping, as a waitress, a bartender, front desk...there wasn't much in the service industry she hadn't done. It wasn't the tasks at Chatsworth Manor that she found difficult, not at all. It was feeling like she was "Mary's daughter" rather than simple Esme Flanagan. Not everyone took her seriously.

"But your mum...she's going to be okay?"

Esme smiled, though it felt wobbly. There was real concern in Stephen's voice, which she appreciated. She liked to think her mum was more than just a housekeeper to him. Esme and Stephen had scampered into the kitchen often enough after school, looking for snacks. Her mum had always been around, and while it hadn't been her place to discipline Stephen, exactly, the two of them had known without question that any bad behavior would result in Esme being in trouble with her mum and Stephen would have to pay the piper with Aurora.

"I hope she will be," she whispered, then

cleared her throat. "There are no guarantees, of course. The survival rate for her type of cancer is good, though, over eighty percent. There was some lymph node involvement."

Stephen reached for the plate of cake, then frowned. He took the unused knife on the tray and cut the generous slice down the middle. "Let's share," he said. "Marjorie's sponge is perfection."

She was tempted because he was right. No one did a Victoria Sponge like the cook. But it wouldn't be right. She couldn't sit in the library and share cake off a plate with the Earl of Chatsworth, no matter how long they'd known each other. Her mother would have a fit if she knew they were even chatting in such a casual way. As much as Mary Flanagan adored the Pemberton family, the line between staff and employer was one that she simply did not cross. It had been fine when they'd been kids, but Esme and Stephen were not children any longer. She watched his long fingers as he replaced the knife on the tray. No, indeed. They were not children.

"I should get back to work. While the rest of the family is out of residence, we've been turning out the bedrooms. I've been carrying on while the maids are off."

"It's just cake, Esme."

"And you're the earl, Stephen. We're not eight years old any longer and climbing apple trees after school."

His relaxed expression turned to one of annoyance, as if he wasn't used to being contradicted or turned down for anything. "You were always better at climbing than I was," he admitted.

She half laughed, half snorted, then straightened her face. "I was nimble. But you were always faster on your bicycle."

"Longer legs," he replied, cutting into the cake with the side of his fork.

Not that she'd ever breathe a word of it, but she found his height quite attractive. There was something about a tall man that was so alluring. At five-eight, she appreciated a man who would still be a little taller than her, even if she were in heels.

Which was altogether silly as she wore very practical black shoes at work, and they would not be seeing each other anywhere other than in the house. And the conversation had taken a turn into a trip down memory lane, which was even more inappropriate. She stood, knowing she needed to go. Get back to her job…the one he was paying her to do.

"Mmm. I have missed this." He closed his eyes as he chewed and swallowed the first bite of cake. He speared a piece on his fork and held it out. "Come on, Esme. One bite won't kill you."

One bite, from the fork that had just been in his mouth. Something delicious swirled in her stomach at the thought. He was acting as if it was nothing at all, but to her it felt intimate. She absolutely shouldn't. But he gave the fork a small wiggle and she gave in, leaned forward, and closed her lips around the tines.

The soft sponge and sweet jam mingled in her mouth, and she closed her eyes for a moment. She didn't eat cake anymore. Didn't eat a lot of things, and for a lot of reasons. But the single bite was heaven, and she let herself enjoy it and the moment, as neither could happen again.

"See? Delicious. You should have brought two forks."

She swallowed and forced a smile. "It is delicious. And now I really do need to get back to work. First of all, I need to ensure your room is ready for you, since you weren't expected."

His smile faded and was replaced by a look she interpreted as annoyed. Well, one of them had to be sensible. One bite of cake off his fork and her heart was hammering. He was the stereotypical tall, dark, and handsome man, and he had a title. That would have been enough to make her a little awestruck. But having history with him? That just made things worse. And she would absolutely not be foolish during the next two weeks.

"Of course." He took his cue from her and the officious-looking mask fell over his face again, almost as if the little moment of familiarity had never happened. "I will be working in here for the remainder of the afternoon. I'll expect dinner at seven and tomorrow morning I'll have breakfast at eight. The garden designer will be here at nine to go over the plans."

"Of course. I'll make sure to have everything on time. Will you be wanting a coffee service for the meeting?"

"That would be really nice, actually. Thank you."

"It's my job," she said simply. Only right now she was looking at being housekeeper, housemaid, and cook all in one.

It took all she had not to affect a little curtsy before leaving as she knew he'd hate it. Actually, knowing that tempted her a little more, but she showed restraint. "I'll come back for your tray shortly. Enjoy your cake. And just ring if you need more coffee."

She turned to leave the room and made herself drop her shoulders and try to relax. What was it about Stephen Pemberton that both put her on edge but also made her feel so at home?

As she pulled the door shut behind her with a solid click, she sighed. Her role here at the manor had always been a bit of a paradox. Daughter of staff, but friend of the eldest child. And right now, that made her feel as if she really didn't belong anywhere.

CHAPTER TWO

IT WAS TEN o'clock before the garden designer left Stephen in the library, now the recipient of sets of plans for the rather ambitious "traditional English garden" that Aurora had commissioned. The designer came highly recommended and was one of the best in the country, having recently worked on the team that had created the sunken garden at Kensington Palace. As far as Stephen knew, he was just there to approve things and make sure everyone got paid. Both things he could have accomplished from Paris, but it was becoming increasingly clear that his mother—and perhaps the rest of the family—had wanted him out of their hair for a while.

Not that he didn't care about the garden…he did. It was in honor of his father and since his death, the family had come close to falling apart more than once. And it had been up to Stephen to lead them through it.

Stephen's hands stilled on the plans as he considered the last few months. He was so weary of carrying the load of being earl and eldest son. Just when everything had started to come together— Bella and Burke, and then Christophe marrying Sophie, and everyone adjusting to new roles at Aurora, Inc., drama and scandal had struck yet again. He was still trying to work through his feelings about having a half-sister only six months younger than William and Charlotte. He tried and tried to reconcile the man he'd known as his father with the man who had stepped out on his wife, fathered a child, and kept it all secret for nearly thirty years. Who was Cedric Pemberton? Stephen felt he needed to know, because until their half-sister, Anemone, had arrived in their lives, Stephen had made it his mission to emulate his father's perfection. With that image shattered, he felt rather adrift—particularly in his role as the current earl. It was hard to know what to do next.

He certainly didn't think his father's mistake should erase all the other wonderful memories or deeds, though. It only proved Cedric had been human. But Stephen was torn about his father's hypocrisy. The man had instilled the importance of honesty and integrity in his children from the time they were walking. Knowing he hadn't followed those same principles left Stephen with unanswered questions and a hefty amount of resentment.

"You look as if you're carrying the weight of the world on your shoulders."

He looked up from the plans and saw Esme standing just inside the door, carrying a tray with the ubiquitous coffeepot, freshly filled.

"Not the world." The words came out clipped, and he let out a sigh. "Sorry. Maybe I'm carrying a small part of it, though."

She came forward and put down the tray. "I won't disturb you," she said. "Ring if you need anything else."

Stephen lifted his hand and ran it along the back of his neck. "Actually, there is something you could do for me."

Esme turned back to him, her green eyes alight with curiosity. "Yes?"

"Come for a ride with me." The moment the words were out of his mouth, he knew a ride throughout the estate was just what he needed. "It's been months since I was on horseback. I've been cooped up in an office."

"I have a job to do. If you don't want to go out alone, maybe one of the grooms would go with you."

He knew it wasn't right to put a staff member in this position. But this was Esme. She was different. It surprised him to realize he'd been longing for a friendly face. One with no agenda and no complications.

"You used to go out riding with me all the time."

"When we were ten. It isn't exactly the same,

sir—I mean, Stephen." She lifted her chin. "My mother would have a canary if I did such a thing."

"Why?" he asked, truly curious about her answer. But she remained silent, her mouth set in a stubborn line. It annoyed him. Not because he was used to having his orders followed, but because she seemed so determined to make a lot out of their differences. He frowned. Goodness, she didn't think he was a snob, did she?

"You know why," she replied quietly. "I'm sorry, Stephen. I can't go riding with you today. But I will send word to the stables to have one of the horses tacked for you."

"It would be nicer with company."

"I'm sure all you'd have to do is pick up the phone and you could have all the company you would ever want."

Was that a hint of jealousy in her voice? Or just disdain? Either way, he liked it. Not because he enjoyed winding her up, necessarily, or arguing. But because despite the power differential between them, which she annoyingly kept bringing up, she was not afraid to voice an opinion. It would be no fun at all if she simply answered everything with "yes, sir, right away, sir" which was what he often got in Paris at Aurora headquarters.

"I could," he admitted, replying to her last statement. "But it would be tiresome and…work. Being social, I mean. And worse, someone might read something into it."

She laughed then, a light, surprised sound. "So I'm not tiresome? Or work?" She lifted an eyebrow. "And you don't think people would read something into it if I spent an afternoon out riding with you?"

God, he loved how she challenged him. It was invigorating. "Who would? There's no one here. And if I must be here, doing all the earl-like things, it might be nice to know I have a friend nearby."

Her face softened as she came a little closer, peering up at him with her startling green eyes. "Are you lonely, Stephen?"

He made a sound that came out like "Pssht."

"Of course not. I'm just looking for something low-key and comfortable." But her question came a little too close to the mark. Lonely wasn't quite the right word, but he wasn't sure what was. He just knew that this bit of banter with her made him forget all his other worries for half a minute.

"Well, you'll have to be low-key by yourself. I have work to do. Since you're paying me to do it and all."

"I could command you to go. As your employer." The moment the words left his mouth he regretted them.

"But you won't," she said easily. "It's not your style. Oh, I think some people think it is, but it's not, not really. Go. Have your ride. It'll be good for thinking."

"I shall." He wouldn't let her refusal deter him, even as he mentally thought backward to the last time someone had refused him anything.

It was quite possibly his non-wedding to Gabi. Was he really that intimidating?

She left then, and he went to the coffee tray and poured himself a cup. There was a little plate with biscuits, too, and he smiled to himself. The biscuits on the plate weren't from the Pemberton kitchen. They were a particular favorite of his that came out of a package. Hobnobs, Esme had called them when she'd once packed a basket for the two of them. He had been seven, she six, and they were planning to run away from home because Mrs. Flanagan and his mother had said that Esme could not take music lessons with him. They'd both been livid at the injustice of it all, particularly Stephen who did not want music lessons to begin with. He had come up with the plan to run away and Esme had said she would provide the food, and so the basket had contained her favorite foods: peanut butter sandwiches, a thermos of chocolate milk, and a sleeve of chocolate-covered Hobnobs.

They'd made it all the way into the village when Cedric had finally found them. Stephen had been afraid he was going to get into huge trouble, but Cedric sat beside them at the town square, thoughtfully ate a peanut butter sandwich, and said he expected they should get home as Mrs. Flanagan was bound to be worried about Esme.

Stephen wondered now if his father hadn't understood that urge to run away from all the rules and expectations. Now he could never ask him. Or ask him if his affair had been the result of rebelling against his restrictive life.

All Stephen knew was that he wouldn't make the same mistake.

The August day was hot but not overly so; the sunshine felt glorious on his face and soaked through the fabric of his shirt while the muscles of the animal beneath him shifted rhythmically in an easy gallop. The saddle was familiar and yet not; it had been too long since he'd taken an afternoon to go riding. He eased his seat a little, slowing his mount until they reached a walk, and then reached down and gave the gelding's neck a pat. No sense overheating the animal just because he was feeling the need to blow off some steam.

The park surrounding Chatsworth Manor was nothing short of splendid, consisting of rolling green hills, leafy trees and a brook leading to a pond where he now took his horse for a drink. He dismounted and hooked the reins around his hand, walking forward, breathing in the rarefied air and marveling at the quiet surrounding him. There was nothing but the whisper of wind in the trees and the sweet chirping of birdsong in the bushes. No traffic. No chatter or phones ringing. Occasionally the odd sound of an airplane overhead. But mostly…peace. Tranquility.

He wished Esme had come with him, but thinking about it now, he knew she was right in that it had probably been wrong to ask. They weren't children anymore. And it wasn't that she was an employee, either, though she was correct that it could make things awkward. It was more this moment, and the solitude, and realizing how intimate it would be with two people, far away from the house or any other eyes. She inspired a comfort in him that was highly unusual at this point in his life, simply because she'd known him as a child. But what did that mean, really? He would be foolish to trust her—to let her in—based solely on their past association as children. Besides, was that what he really wanted? It wouldn't be fair to use her as a diversion.

Now that he was here at the manor house, he was beginning to realize he needed to face some things head-on. And as a man who'd made an art form of controlling his feelings, the thought of giving his emotions some control was terrifying. He didn't trust it. Come to think of it, he didn't trust anyone or anything these days. He suspected that was a great deal of the problem.

As his horse dipped his head to the pond, Stephen rolled his shoulders. Ah yes, trust. It apparently worked for some people, but it certainly never had for him. He'd trusted Bridget—he'd loved her, for God's sake—but she'd betrayed him horribly. And he'd trusted his friendship with Gabi, even if their engagement had been a sham, and she'd left him at the altar. Even family…look at Anemone. Her whole arrival at Aurora in Paris had been based on false pretenses, not to mention the greatest lie of all—her paternity, which his parents had both known about and never revealed.

People let people down. That was all there was to it.

Now he was supposed to be thrilled to be supervising this massive undertaking for a garden and fountain to honor his father when he had so many conflicting feelings he wanted to wash his hands of the whole responsibility.

Maybe Esme was right. Maybe he was lonely.

He tilted his neck to either side, trying to release the tension there. His mother had "suggested" the trip as a way to relax. But all the relaxing was doing was making him think too much. And the thinking made him feel things—uncomfortable things. Like anger and frustration.

As the sun soaked into his skin, he let out a gigantic sigh. What he really wanted to do was escape this life for a day. No, more like a week. Pretend he wasn't an earl, wasn't the COO at Aurora, Inc., pretend he was an ordinary bloke with ordinary responsibilities.

Except…he wasn't ordinary, and never would

be. From the time he'd turned thirteen and he'd been sent off to school, he'd been groomed for this life. He'd never had a choice. And it had never bothered him very much…until now.

His horse was sufficiently rested, so he swung back up into the saddle again and adjusted the reins in his hands. His afternoon pity party was at an end. Because back at the house all his responsibilities waited, and he felt the burden of them as he spurred his mount and moved forward.

Esme watched Stephen lead his horse back to the stables and held back a sigh of appreciation.

His long legs, his great butt… Buff-colored riding breeches disappeared into riding boots, and he wore a white polo shirt, which contrasted with his muscled, tanned arms. His stride was long and easy, and her mouth went dry as he walked through the garden. She'd stepped outside to check the moisture levels in the herb pots when he'd returned from his ride. She was sorry now that she'd refused his invitation, no matter how improper it would have been. Oh, it wasn't even the impropriety. She wasn't *that* stiff. It was the shocking discovery that the silly schoolgirl crush she'd started developing just before he'd gone away hadn't been as silly as she'd once thought. It had flickered to life again on his arrival, and with every encounter it flared just a little bit brighter. How embarrassing. How…

Well. If she were being honest—only with herself—it was rather surprising and not entirely unwelcome. Her ability to feel attraction had been rather dead for quite some time, and she was only thirty-four. It came as something of a relief to realize that part of her still worked. For a very long time, she'd thought her marriage and subsequent divorce from Evan had killed it stone dead.

But Stephen? Ridiculous. For one thing, he was the earl. He was stupid rich, and lived in Paris most of the year, and ran in the same circles as celebrities and VIPs.

That didn't mean she couldn't admire the package, however. And it was a very fine package.

She went back inside, knowing she needed to get back to work. There was an evening meal to plan—that she had to cook—and other duties on her list that needed checking off. Esme had planned to take this week to catch up on random tasks that were done on more of a quarterly or annual basis.

She was counting linens when Stephen's voice interrupted her.

"You're still here."

She jumped, losing count. Her pulse thrummed at the sound of his voice, especially since she'd been thinking about him. This was a big house, but perhaps it wasn't going to be big enough for the next few weeks.

But she schooled her features and nodded. "I

am. I'll be here until after dinner." She'd set some short ribs to braise an hour ago and intended to make garlic mash and glazed vegetables to go with it. Thankfully last night Stephen had mentioned that he didn't normally eat pudding so there was no need for desserts while he was home. Esme was a decent cook, but there was no way she could bake like Marjorie.

"After dinner…" He frowned, and then his eyebrows shot up as if he'd just come to the correct conclusion. "No other staff. You're doing it all. Including the cooking?"

She nodded. "It's no trouble. I like to cook. Though I can't compare to Marjorie."

"Last night's roast chicken was delicious."

"Well, thank you. Anyway yes, I'll head home after the tidying up." And then worry about her own dinner, and washing dishes, and getting up in time to be back here to start his breakfast. Oh, and checking in on Mum. Because now that she was doing chemo, the side effects were more worrisome.

"My being here has definitely caused an imposition," he said, his voice low. "I'm sorry."

"How can it be an imposition if it's my job?" she asked. "You're paying me to do it."

She realized how sharp she sounded, and it wasn't what she intended at all. Here she was trying to not be overly friendly—to maintain the boundaries that needed to be maintained—and instead she just sounded…crabby.

"It's a very long day for you, that's all." He pursed his lips. "Esme, at home I fend for myself quite often. I can do so here, as well. Especially for breakfast." He shrugged. "I can make coffee. And toast. And even fry an egg."

"It's not necessary…" She looked away, feeling oddly embarrassed. Would he give someone else the same consideration? Or was it just because it was…her? There was no way she would ask. She felt strange about it already.

"Suit yourself." He took a step back, his face closed off again. "However, I can certainly eat earlier than seven. So you're not so late getting home."

He was being kind, making adjustments, and she was being…not herself. She didn't know how to act around him anymore, and that made her sad. She thought back to all the years as children when they'd actually finished each other's sentences. This was what they'd become. But what if it could be different? What if they could be… friends? Did she even want that?

"I'm sorry," she offered, softening her voice. "I've been short with you, putting boundaries in place because of, well, who we grew up to be. I don't mean to be off-putting."

"Maybe it would be better if we just said what we mean," he replied, shoving his hands in his pockets. It made him look a little bit boyish, and she responded to that.

That was the problem. She responded to him, and she didn't want to, and there was no way in the world she could say it to his face.

Then he surprised her.

"Would it help if I said that I am absolutely not looking for any big complication, that I remember our time as children fondly, and I would like to spend my time here relaxed around each other?"

Could she manage "relaxed"?

She lifted her chin. "Actually, that helps a great deal, because I feel exactly the same way."

He let out a breath. "Good. Then let's agree to call each other by first names, and perhaps in the days ahead I'll do my work and you can do yours, but we might actually be able to hold a conversation without tensing up and wondering if being friendly crosses some sort of invisible line."

Esme met his gaze, ignoring the jolt that went right to her toes with the eye contact. "As a friend, I'd appreciate moving the dinner time by an hour. That means I can check on Mum on my way home."

"And if you need time for any reason, to take your mum to appointments or anything, please take it. I know I'm…authoritative. But I'm not an ogre." A smile ghosted his lips. "Despite what my siblings might say."

"Surely they don't—"

"Oh, they do," he said, cutting off her protest. "And if I'm honest, I deserve the criticism. At least some of it."

She wondered why. Wondered what had changed, where the fun-loving boy had gone. Though she rather suspected that beneath that cool veneer was a man who cared about things very deeply. What she didn't understand was why he kept that side of himself under lock and key.

And that thought took her way past "friendly" yet again. That simple request was going to be the hardest to follow.

Stephen tapped a long finger against his top lip. Esme couldn't help but follow the path of it. The shadow of the day's stubble already darkened his jaw, even though he'd been clean-shaven for his meeting this morning. She wondered if it was prickly or soft.

"I suppose it would cross a line to ask you to join me for dinner tonight?"

Both responses—*it would* and *of course not*—flitted through her brain. As if sensing her hesitation, he lifted a shoulder in a shrug. "It's a bit lonely, sitting in the dining room all by myself. And you have to eat, too. There's no reason why you shouldn't fix a plate and join me."

She gave up. While she had her reasons for putting space between them that went beyond the simple employer/employee relationship, she couldn't deny he was making sense and she was creating friction where there didn't need to be any.

"Fine, I will," she answered. "But before I can do that, I need to finish counting these linens."

He nodded. "And I have some estate things to go over in the library."

"Then I guess I'll see you in the dining room at…six?" It sounded ridiculously early, considering the family usually ate at seven thirty or eight. But he nodded and offered a small smile.

"Six is perfect," he said, and before she could catch her breath, he turned on his heel and disappeared.

CHAPTER THREE

STEPHEN PULLED OPEN the heavy wood door that marked the entrance to The Tilted Lizard. He was immediately treated to the sound of fiddly folk music and the smell of chips and beer. Inside the door, behind the hostess lectern, was a carving of a gecko, leaning sideways on a cattail and wearing a broad grin. Stephen laughed. It was ridiculous and perfect all at once.

He scanned the pub for a seat but instead of an empty table, he saw Esme.

Lord, she was beautiful. It hit him like a ton of bricks every time he saw her. Last night, sitting with her in the dining room over a delicious meal, he'd loosened up and actually smiled and joked a little. It was impossible to remain immune to her easy charm and smile. The way her face lit up seemed to warm him from the inside out. And sure, it had been a little awkward at first, but they'd relaxed over a single glass of wine with their food. It had only lasted thirty minutes, but she'd opened up a bit about her mother's illness, and he'd responded with similar worries after Maman's heart scare at Gabi and Will's wedding, the parental worry providing common ground between them.

One of the staff had stopped by her table. Esme said something and gestured with her hands while the other woman nodded enthusiastically, and then they both laughed. He swore he could hear the lilting sound through the rest of the din, and his heart gave a solid thump in response. She was so animated, so utterly lovely with her easy smile. It was a revelation. Since he'd arrived only a few days ago, and with the exception of dinner last night, she'd been so uptight, so reserved. It had worried him, wondering why she'd changed so much from the girl he remembered. Clearly she was at home here in the pub, as her face was relaxed and her smile easy—in a way it wasn't with him.

He wondered why.

Regardless, he certainly didn't want to encroach on her evening. He'd find somewhere else to have a pint. Maybe. He wasn't exactly spoiled for choice in the village. He was about to turn back to the door when her gaze lifted, and she saw him there. Immediately heat rose to his cheeks. To leave now without at least saying hello would be rude, and he'd been surly enough over the past few days. So he gave a little wave and started forward, pretending that he hadn't just got caught staring at her.

He reached her table and offered a smile, though

his usual protocol of social greeting made him nearly lean forward to kiss her cheek. Totally not appropriate in this situation, so instead he offered a hello to the waitress as he pulled out a chair.

"Sandy, this is Stephen. Stephen, Sandy. Sandy and I used to work together."

"And get into trouble together," Sandy offered, sending a wink in their general direction. Stephen liked her already.

"Interesting. Same here. Getting into trouble, I mean."

Sandy hadn't put together who he was, for which he was grateful. "Oh?"

"I've known Stephen since I was a kid."

"And when we got in trouble, I always took the blame."

"You always offered," Esme retorted, but her eyes twinkled in a way they hadn't since he'd shown up at the manor.

"It was the gentlemanly thing to do," he replied.

Sandy was chuckling. "Es has already ordered her drink, but what can I get you?"

He would have taken a whiskey, but he wondered if that would be too…well, predictable. "What do you recommend that's on tap?"

"Depends on what you like."

"I'll have a pint of an IPA…surprise me, Sandy."

"Ooh, an adventurous type." She waggled her eyebrows at Esme as she smiled. Esme just rolled her eyes. "Back in a flash," Sandy said, spinning about and walking away with an extra jut of her hip.

"That girl..." Esme shook her head and laughed. "We've had some good times together."

"She seems fun."

"She is. Young yet. Though her latest boyfriend might just make her want to settle down." The words were infused with skepticism, and Stephen had the fleeting thought that Esme was soured on romance. He certainly understood that.

"That's not for you, though?" Stephen found himself curious to learn a little more about Esme's past. It wasn't like any details ever got filtered from the household staff to the family. He hadn't even known Mrs. Flanagan was ill, and the last he'd heard mention of Esme... He wracked his brain. He seemed to remember Mrs. Flanagan saying something in passing a few years ago about a divorce. Had Esme been married? And what fool had been stupid enough to let her go?

She shrugged. "I thought it was, once."

He snorted. "Yeah, me too. Not anymore, though."

His reply caused an awkward silence, which Esme thankfully covered. "So," Esme said, "what brings you to The Tilted Lizard?"

"I came in search of a pint and some noise. The house is very quiet when you're in it all alone."

"You don't strike me as the social type."

He chuckled a little. "To be honest, I like the background noise. I don't need to be social."

Her cheeks colored a little and he hurriedly covered his gaffe. "Present company doesn't count. I don't mean to intrude on your evening."

"You're not. My best friend is supposed to be joining me for a few drinks, but she's running late. But I understand if you'd rather be alone. You won't hurt my feelings if you want to sit at the bar."

Now he felt like an ass. "I don't mind keeping you company for a while if you don't. I mean, until your friend gets here."

"I don't mind." She smiled a little, almost shyly, which did a strange little something to his chest.

Her gaze swept over him, and her eyes lit with approval as she nodded at his jeans and casual button-down. "No Savile Row in sight."

"No, not tonight." Tonight he'd dressed far more casual than normal.

She leaned over and looked under the table, then back up at him. "Well, except the Italian leather. Those give you away."

"They're my favorite shoes," he explained.

"Don't you have trainers? Something that at least looks a little scuffed?"

"Trainers are for the gym." He sat back as Sandy returned with their drinks. "Thank you, Sandy."

"Shall I start a tab? Do you know what you'd like for dinner?"

"You know what I'm having," Esme said.

"Two pieces cod and chips, hold the tartar, extra vinegar," Sandy supplied.

Esme beamed.

Sandy looked at Stephen. "We've got a steak sandwich on special tonight, served with chips or mash. Also our signature dish, Bangers and Smashed. Two sausages, garlic mash, veg of the day and a glass of beer."

Heart attack on a plate, both of them. He looked at Esme and back at Sandy. "As much as Bangers and Smashed sounds amazing, it's just the beer for me, thanks. I ate earlier." Esme had been off the hook for cooking tonight, as he'd set up meetings in London and he'd grabbed something before driving back.

Sandy looked at Esme and grinned, hooking a thumb in Stephen's direction. "He's all right," she said, and then scooted away again.

Esme put down her glass and looked up at him. "Did you really come here for background noise?"

He took another drink of beer before putting down his glass. Esme was staring at him expectantly, and all he could do was think about how pretty she was in her faded jeans and cute top. It was tomato-red with a scoop neck and a little tie at the throat that she'd left undone. The color should have clashed with her hair, but it didn't. Hoop earrings were in her ears, too—the kind that she apparently didn't wear to work at the estate.

"I did. I've been thinking about what you said the other day, about the possibility that I'm lonely. It's entirely possible. Though perhaps instead of lonely, solitary is a better word."

She smiled softly. "You aren't comfortable in your own company, but you don't want anything intimate, either. Don't let anyone close, but don't spend so much time by yourself that you overthink everything."

He stared at her.

"What?" she asked. "Did you think you were the only one in the world to feel that way?"

He bristled a little on the inside, both because she'd verbalized exactly how he was feeling and because she'd accurately pointed out that this was not his unique circumstance, and he felt a bit embarrassed.

"Listen, I'm not trying to elicit any sympathy, but the life I lead…it's one of expectations."

"As the Earl of Chatsworth."

"Yes, as the earl. And in my position as COO. And the eldest child. And the one to follow in my father's footsteps. My father who—"

He stopped himself before he got carried away and said too much. He'd been trying to carry the load of, well, everything for months now, living up to an ideal he no longer believed in. It surprised him to realize he was actually quite angry about that. "Anyway, seeing you the last few days reminded me what it was like when I was younger. Before expectations and obligations and, well, consequences. At least big consequences. Esme, I don't actually remember the last time I had fun."

She took a drink of beer. "That's pathetic. What happened, you inherited the title and automatically got a stick up your butt?"

He burst out laughing and oh, it felt good. She'd surprised him but there was joy in the feeling that expanded his chest and sent the laugh out of his mouth. This was the Esme he remembered. The one who said exactly what she thought and called him out on his bull. Yes, it had been strained around the house, but tonight he loved that she was treating him as no one special. "Oh, Esme. I haven't laughed like that in a long time."

"You really are in need of an intervention. I think it's going to take more than a pint and some footy on the telly."

"You might be right. Maman sent me back here, ostensibly to oversee the garden plans, but I could have done that from Paris. She really sent me to take a vacation and get out of everyone's hair. I've become a bit of a grump."

"I believe you used the word *ogre*."

"You certainly express your opinion much more freely here than at the manor," he observed. It wasn't a criticism. He was rather enjoying her teasing. Most people just stared at him and avoided eye contact.

Her face flattened, though. "Oh, I'm sorry. Truly. I was teasing but not if it cuts a little too close."

"It doesn't. It's refreshing. Besides, Maman is right, though I won't admit it to her face. I needed to get away. I need to…figure a few things out." And he hated it. Navel-gazing and sorting through feelings was so not his thing.

Her face softened and she reached out and touched his hand. "What is it? Is it work? Or is it the estate? It must be so hard without your father. I know how you idolized him."

"I suppose it's all of that." He considered telling her about Anemone, but that *trust* word popped up again, and he avoided the subject. "It's like running two businesses, really. The estate interests and Aurora's, as well. And while I was a part of both for the past several years—"

"It's different when you're the one everyone looks to. When it's your signature on the bottom line."

He nodded. They both sat back as a different server brought Esme's food and set it before her, as well as another beer for Stephen. "Sandy says she thinks you'll like this brew." The young woman smiled as she put down the glass.

"Thanks, Sarah." Esme smiled up at the server.

"And another for me, please." She gestured at the near-empty glass.

She looked up at Stephen. "I live just down the road. No need for me to drive."

She reached for the cruet and drizzled her fish with the tangy vinegar. "So," she said, reaching for a bottle of brown sauce and putting some on her plate. "What I'm hearing is the Pemberton version of *'Heavy lies the head that wears the crown'.*"

She wasn't wrong. "It's that predictable, is it?"

Esme shook her head. "No, I suppose not. But I know firsthand that trying to live up to someone else's expectations is a sure way to set yourself up for failure."

He stared at her as she dipped a chip in the sauce and popped it into her mouth.

Esme couldn't believe she'd actually said that out loud. The last thing she needed was for Stephen to start asking questions. He certainly didn't need to hear about her crash-and-burn marriage to Evan, and how she'd turned herself inside out trying to be what he wanted. And yeah, maybe she'd known Stephen longer, but the simple fact remained: he, and Evan, too, lived in a different world from her.

The piece of fish she'd stabbed with her fork fell off the tines and back onto the plate. "Sorry," she offered weakly. "I might have been projecting a bit there."

Stephen put down his beer. "You're right, though. I have never not been either the earl or the heir or the firstborn or part of the business. The time we had as kids…that was as close to normal as my childhood ever got." He sat back in his chair and met her gaze. "My upbringing was ridiculously privileged. And I'm lucky, I know that. But I'm afraid it's also turned me into someone who isn't much fun and lives in a constant state of stress so pervasive that I don't know what it would feel like to not have it."

"So…you going off to school. Is that why you never…?" She hesitated. "Why you disappeared?"

"I came home for holidays. But suddenly I was no longer a child—I was the future heir training to take my place. I don't know how else to explain it."

She knew she shouldn't say it, but she couldn't help herself. "And a friendship with me didn't fit in that place."

His cheeks pinkened a little bit. "It's not…well, maybe it is. I was thirteen. You were twelve. Us running wild over the estate was suddenly not the done thing." He put air quotes around the last, as if someone had said those exact words to him. "And I think it had nothing to do with you or where you come from and everything to do with me leaving childish things behind and growing up."

While she understood the sentiment, she balked at the words "childish things." Their friendship had been her mainstay. Cedric Pemberton had been the closest thing to a father she'd ever had, and Stephen her best friend.

"I understand," she said, picking at her battered cod. "But I was horribly adrift after you left. Nothing was the same."

She probably shouldn't have admitted that, and she couldn't make herself look at him. She was too embarrassed. But then his hand was warm on hers, sending tingles to her fingertips and a fluttering sensation to her belly.

She should not be this aware of Stephen Pemberton.

"I'm sorry," he said softly, just loud enough that she could hear it over the sound of the other patrons. "If it helps, I missed our friendship, too."

There was that word again. *Friends.* She regained her composure and slid her hand away from his, then picked up her fork again, taking a bite of the fish. The golden batter was perfection, the fish fresh, the vinegar adding just the right tang. When she'd finished her mouthful, she was steady enough to look at him again.

He looked absolutely contrite, the hard lines of his face softened as he looked at her. "I should have made more of an effort."

She tried a smile. "We were kids. It's all right. I just didn't have a lot of friends. I'd always had you. And the house wasn't the same without you in it, either. Bella was nice to me, but it wasn't the same."

She pushed away her plate, no longer hungry. Where the heck was Phoebe, anyway? She should have been here an hour ago. A quick check of her phone showed she'd missed a text. "Looks like my friend got held up. She should be here soon, though."

What she didn't say was how she'd really felt when he'd been sent away. She'd felt invisible, like she wasn't important, and that she wasn't good enough to be his friend. And she deeply regretted the argument they'd had just before he'd gone off to school, where she'd thrown his title in his face. It didn't matter that she'd been twelve. She'd been hurt and she'd lashed out, and so who could blame him for not coming back?

At least with Evan it had been different. She'd had the same feelings—of not being good enough, and often invisible. Definitely criticized. But she'd been the one to do the walking. And she had no regrets except that it had taken her so long to get up the gumption to go.

"But you finished school here. And then?" he asked, prompting her.

"Nothing so glamorous as Aurora or aristocracy. I didn't know what I wanted to do in school, so I started working. And then…well, the pay is terrible, but I actually love my job. I manage housekeeping at the inn. I've worked in just about every position there, and hospitality suits me. I love welcoming people and making sure their experience is special."

"And is there a husband? A boyfriend?" He looked at her more closely. "Girlfriend? I don't want to presume."

"No boyfriend, no girlfriend, and a *was*-band." She rolled her eyes. "We divorced four years ago."

"And no kids."

"No."

"Well, I suppose that makes cutting ties slightly easier. I'm sorry, though."

She shook her head. "Don't be. I'm far happier now." She took a sip of her beer. "And I know you're single. Unless you have a girlfriend hiding away from the paparazzi."

Stephen made a noise that was somewhere between a scoff and a snort. "No girlfriend. Two failed attempts at the altar means I'm not in any sort of rush to try again."

There was an awkward silence, and then Esme bravely held up her glass. "A toast then, to Evan and Bridget and Gabi. Their loss."

He stared at her, a stunned expression in his eyes. "You know their names."

"One word, Stephen. Tabloids."

He muttered something incomprehensible, but she caught his meaning and grinned, then waited for him to tap his glass to hers. He did, they drank, and she settled back in her chair, feeling better somehow. Talking to him tonight had been good, and perhaps easier because they were on neutral territory.

"I should be on my way," Stephen said, interrupting her thoughts. "There are still some aspects of the estate that aren't settled. The solicitor is coming tomorrow. I do have to prepare a few things."

It was a paltry excuse and they both knew it. It was unlikely he'd go back home now and stay up to do paperwork. Perhaps the conversation that made her feel better had been more uncomfortable for him.

"Let me know what time, and I'll make sure to have a coffee service for you."

"Thank you, Esme." He got up from his chair, but suddenly crouched down, one hand braced on the table and the other touching her knee with the barest of touches. "Esme, I am sorry about your divorce, and I'm sorry that our friendship was a casualty of my... I don't even know what to call it. It sounds horrible to complain when I have everything a person could ever want, but good friends are a rare find. We should never be careless with them."

She swallowed and nodded, touched, unsure of what to say, feeling the ridiculous urge to tip just a little bit forward and kiss him. Kiss him! What a foolish idea. Especially since that *friend* word just kept cropping up over and over again. He couldn't be more clear about where he stood.

"I'll see you at the house tomorrow," she said instead, and he gave her a brief nod.

"Yes, tomorrow."

"Thank you for the company," she offered, feeling both relief and sadness that he was leaving.

"Thank you," he replied, and bestowed a rare smile on her. "You're much nicer than background noise from the telly."

And then he was gone.

CHAPTER FOUR

ESME REFILLED THE coffeepot and prepared to take it to the library, where Stephen was meeting with his solicitor. She'd baked some sugar biscuits this morning and added them to the tray, making sure they were arranged prettily on the plate. Then she lifted it all, took a breath, and stepped out of the kitchen.

She'd already seen Stephen after his breakfast. She'd arrived promptly at eight, planning to fix him something to eat, only to find he'd already made himself scrambled eggs and toast. The jeans and button-down from the night before were nowhere to be seen. Instead, he was in one of his pristine suits, this time in a charcoal grey with a blue shirt and striped tie.

Every inch the earl, even if he had fried his own eggs.

The end result had Esme feeling off balance. Last night she'd thought more about Evan than she had in months. And it wasn't that she was bitter; it was more that she didn't like who she'd become during the years she'd spent with him. At first, she'd been taken in by his charms. His family had taken a house nearby for a year while his father commuted to London. He'd been home from university for an extended vacation and he and some of his mates had booked into the inn for a week, using it as a base while they got up to… well, all sorts of things. She'd been cleaning rooms at the time, and there were always bottles to pick up the morning after, but Evan had been a great tipper and had a way of smiling at her whenever they crossed paths. His friends had departed, but Evan still found reasons to pop round the hotel. And Esme had been swept off her feet, like Cinderella at a ball.

He'd finished university, proposed, and after the wedding they'd moved to the city for four long years. Four years in which Esme didn't work. Evan didn't want his wife doing menial labor. She was better than that, he said.

And so her years of being isolated had begun.

She shook her head, trying to rid herself of the memories and the heavy feeling they evoked, and approached the library door. She heard Stephen's voice, and another man's answering it. Granted, Stephen didn't seem to look down his nose at what she did for a living, but the fact that they were from two very different worlds was painfully obvious.

She entered the library on soft feet and left the tray on a side table.

"Thank you, Esme." Stephen halted his conversation to acknowledge her, and her cheeks heated.

"Let me know if you need anything else, sir." She added the *sir* simply because he was with someone. It felt odd, though. This was his fourth day here and already they were being consistently familiar with each other.

He found her later, still in the kitchen. She was rolling out pastry for this evening's beef Wellington when he entered. His hair looked as if he'd run his fingers through it several times, and his movements seemed slightly agitated—stiff and uncomfortable.

"Is something wrong?" she asked.

He rolled his shoulders. "Too much coffee, maybe? I don't know." He sighed. "I hate dealing with the will and estate, and it winds me up a bit, I suppose."

She stopped rolling and looked up. "You're still dealing with that? But your father…" She let the sentence trail off. Cedric had been gone for over two years. She'd naturally assumed the terms of the will had been settled long ago.

"With Anemone's appearance, we decided as a family to have another look at Dad's will, find a way for Anemone to get a share. The decision was a family one. The execution of it is up to me and the legal firm to sort through."

Anemone. Ah, yes. The illegitimate daughter. Esme still had a difficult time wrapping her head around the fact that the man she remembered so fondly had had an affair. If she found it difficult to believe, Stephen—and the rest of the family— must have been floored by the revelation.

"It must have been tough for you to learn that about Cedric," she said softly, taking the pâté-topped tenderloin and encasing it in the pastry.

Stephen took a bottle of sparkling water out of the fridge and twisted off the cap. "More than tough. It wasn't just the affair, either." He hesitated, then met her gaze. "It feels strange talking about this outside the family."

"You know nothing goes further than these four walls," Esme assured him. "But if you don't want to talk about it, I understand."

"Actually, no. Maybe it's good that I do."

She stayed silent, waiting.

He pulled up a stool and perched on it, took a drink of the water. "I was the first to find out, you know. Me and the accountant. Dad had been sending her mother money twice a year. I scheduled an audit of the books when I took over the estate and there it was. Then I had to tell the rest of the family."

Esme could only imagine how awful that must have been. "Ouch."

He sighed again. "You know, I guess I felt that it was my responsibility to look out for everyone's interests. To be the steady, objective one. But I had my own feelings to deal with. The man I loved… idolized…and whose footsteps I had to fill, had cheated on my mother and had another child."

"It hurts when our heroes let us down," she whispered.

His gaze held hers. "It does. And I thought I was coming to terms with it all when we found out that Maman knew about Anemone all along. It was like the ground was ripped from beneath my feet."

She slid the Wellington into the refrigerator and washed her hands, then fetched him a glass with some ice for his water, all while absorbing the new information that Lady Pemberton had known of this girl's existence. "But I bet the whole time you told yourself you had to be the steady one. The one who had to look out for the Pemberton best interests."

He nodded. "Apparently I'm a quick study."

"I've known you a long time. As much as we got into scrapes and had fun, you were always looking out for your brother and sisters. Especially Christophe, when he arrived." Christophe was technically Stephen's cousin, though he'd been raised like a brother. More than once, Stephen had stood up for the younger boy at school. He'd stood up for her, too.

He didn't answer, just poured his drink over into the glass.

"So you've been bottling up your feelings about it all this time?"

"Bull's-eye again. And I wasn't very nice to Anemone, who was more of a victim of all this secrecy than anyone."

Esme started picking up her dirty dishes. "Yes, but you couldn't know that."

He was quiet for so long that she stopped and looked up. He was staring at her quite intently, his dark eyes curious. "What?"

"It's just nice that you understand that."

"Listen, I'm a pro at bottling up my feelings and redirecting them elsewhere. The big question is, where has this left you, and why do you walk around with a pained expression on your face all the time that only disappears when you forget it's supposed to be there? Is it guilt? Or stress? Or all of it together?"

He let out a breath with a whoosh. "You know, your mum was always great to talk to when I snuck to the kitchen, but I never felt like I was in a therapy session."

Esme chuckled. "Maybe you should try therapy. It can be quite helpful."

"Personal experience?"

"I walked away from my marriage. It was the first strong thing I'd done in the six years since I met Evan. I had a lot of stuff to unlearn." She could say it matter-of-factly now. But it had been so hard at first. "And," she added, "I wanted to protect Mum from any nastiness, so she really doesn't know about the therapy."

"Maybe you should talk to her about it."

Esme laughed. "She still thinks I was crazy to leave him. And I don't want to argue with her while she's fighting cancer. It's all right."

But she could still relate to how he felt, handling things alone.

He tapped his fingers on the countertop and frowned. "Do I really walk around with a pained expression?"

Esme poured herself her own glass of water and took a sip as she considered him. "Yes. Sometimes your face could frighten small children."

That, at least, made a tiny smile curve the corners of his lips.

"You're unhappy," she said plainly. "And feel as if you don't have a right to be. How close am I?"

"Pretty close."

"And you're soured on love and relationships, because you've crashed and burned, and you probably don't want to a) go through that again, and b) have another Pemberton scandal in the papers."

"Do you charge an hourly rate, doc?"

She laughed again. "Oh, Stephen, it makes so much sense. But heck, understanding the why is the easy part. The healing and moving past it? That's where all the work is. And I can't help you with that. You have to do it yourself. You could maybe start by smiling once in a while and doing something fun."

The way his eyebrow lifted in a skeptical quirk that clearly communicated, "Fun?" made her want to laugh.

"I'm not sure I know where I'd start. Especially here."

"Well, first of all, solitary rides through the countryside and an evening game of billiards in the games room is not fun. You came close last night, though, by popping into the pub. I don't know, go to the gym? Pop into a few shops? There's always a game of something on at the park, either footy or cricket. You might actually meet some people."

He looked so horrified at the idea she cracked up. "Come on, Stephen, I dare you to do something normal."

His jaw tightened and she knew he would agree to something because he couldn't resist a challenge. It was lovely to discover he really hadn't changed all that much. As kids, all she'd had to do was issue a dare, and he'd instantly reacted. If she'd said "Oh, don't go up there, the apples are fine on this branch anyway," he'd taken the bait and climbed to the highest branch. Or if they'd been out on their bicycles, and she'd poked at him with "oh, that hill's too big to bike up anyway," they'd be off to find out what wonders were on the other side. Looking back, it was a wonder they hadn't broken their necks. But it brought back good memories, too. At one time, the memories had been painful, especially when Stephen had gone off to school and she had become a teenager—redheaded, freckled, and awkward. She'd missed those early days horribly, but eventually she'd started to look back on her childhood as a little bit magical. Not every little girl could say they had the run of an English country home when they were small.

Now Stephen was back, too, and knowing that the precocious little boy was still somewhere inside the tall, serious man warmed her heart, made her feel like she hadn't warped the memories over the years.

"So what do you suggest for fun? Shopping and a pickup game of footy isn't really my thing."

She shrugged. "For starters, you could unstarch yourself and dress more casually. Maybe Friday night darts at the pub? There's always a tournament on. And the gooseberry festival is coming up as part of the fair next weekend. There'll be rides and games."

He grimaced. "I have to go anyway. I'm judging some entries or something. My father used to years ago. Apparently this falls under 'duties of the current earl'."

"Oh, darling. That is going to be precious. You, handing out ribbons for gooseberry tarts and jams." She couldn't stop the wide smile that came over her face.

She didn't tell him that her mother entered every year, and this year would be no different, despite Mary's health and cancer treatments. Esme wasn't about to deny her mum the simple pleasure, even if it meant Esme had to help out on top of work.

"Thanks. You're having a little too much fun with this idea."

She got serious again, then, and went to him. She stood on the other side of the counter, facing him, and took one of his hands in hers. It was possibly too familiar a touch, but he'd shared things this morning that had been personal. And he did want to be friends…even if the casual touch of his hand beneath her fingers sent all her senses into overdrive. He didn't need to know that.

"Stephen, my memories of you when we were kids are filled with smiles and laughter and challenges. Where did that boy go?"

"Es…"

The soft way he said the shortened version of her name reached right into her heart and held on.

"You deserve good things too, you know," she continued. "We all do. Loosen up for the next week and leave some of your troubles behind. The world won't end, I promise."

He nodded and cleared his throat, as if he didn't trust himself to speak.

"Now." She brightened her voice, let go of his hand, and broke the moment before it could become uncomfortable. "I have a mess to clean up. And you've spent enough time lollygagging in my kitchen."

"You sound just like your mum when you say that. All right, point taken. I'll get out of your kitchen. Oh, and Esme?"

She'd started running water in the sink for the stack of bowls beside her. "Yes?"

"If I have to ditch the suits, you can ditch the uniform. It's only the two of us here. No more black. Dress in what makes you comfortable."

Her cheeks pinkened. "Oh. Well." She gave a little laugh. "I've been in hotel uniform or black tops and bottoms since I was eighteen, I think."

"Then this will be a change for you, too."

Esme wasn't sure she needed change. After all, she was quite happy with her life as it was. But if she wanted Stephen to step out of his comfort zone, it wasn't unreasonable that he'd request the same. "I'll be sure to dress differently tomorrow, then," she replied.

Stephen left the kitchen and went to the library. He sat at the desk, thinking about his conversation with Esme, then picked up the phone. This was his fourth day here and he hadn't yet touched base with his mother. He knew she was especially invested in the memorial and since they were breaking ground tomorrow, he knew he should call.

The phone rang in his ear and on the third ring she answered. "*Bonjour*, my darling."

"*Bonjour*, Maman," Stephen answered, resting an elbow on his desk. "How are you?"

"Hot." It was August and Aurora had decided to spend the bulk of the summer at the château, traveling to Paris occasionally to see family and pop into Aurora, Inc. headquarters. "It is cool inside, but I cannot seem to get enough of the garden. The lavender is blooming, and the air is gorgeous."

He could picture it and almost wished he were there. There was nothing in the world like Provence.

"Are you expecting company for the weekend?" Often his brothers or sisters would pop down with their significant others or, in Christophe and Charlotte's cases, with grandchildren. He knew Aurora loved that and was adoring being semi-retired.

"Yes. Anemone and Phillipe are visiting. They are planning an October wedding here at the château. Isn't that lovely?"

"It is," he said, his throat tight. He was still getting used to the fact that he had a half-sister. It was…an adjustment.

"I hope they're very happy," he said sincerely. "I know I wasn't necessarily fair to her in the beginning."

"Oh, darling, it is understandable. I wasn't as

open as I should have been with you all, either. It brought back some painful memories for me. But she is here, and she is lovely. At some point I think we must let go of the past."

Something he'd never found easy, and he acknowledged his own resentment that everyone seemed to be able to move beyond it faster than he could. After talking with Esme this morning, he understood it had little to do with Anemone and far more to do with his parents' secrets that he'd inherited along with the title.

"Maman, you were right about me taking a break. I'm still checking on things a little, and keeping an eye on the memorial project, but I've decided to actually use the time here to relax." It was a big thing to admit.

Aurora's rusty laugh, so much like his own, came across the line. "Do you know how, my love?"

He grinned in response, because her laugh could always make him smile. "No. But I've enlisted some help. Esme is caring for the house while Mrs. Flanagan is recuperating. I wish you'd mentioned that, by the way. She didn't even know I was coming."

"She didn't? Oh, *mon Dieu*. I'm sorry. You two used to get into some scrapes as children. I think Mrs. Flanagan ended up using as many plasters on your knees as Esme's." Again came the rusty laugh.

"A lot has changed, Maman. But I'm overdue for some downtime. I don't think I knew how much. I went for a ride and then to a pub for a pint. It felt nice to not be on a tight schedule." Even admitting this felt strange, but necessary. Now that he'd stopped to pause and catch his breath, he realized how he'd buried himself in work to keep from dealing with his personal life.

"Is this my Stephen talking? I don't believe it." After the bit of teasing, Aurora added, "You should enjoy it. You know, I stayed on as CEO for a long time, thinking no one could run Aurora like I could. But when I had my health scare at William's wedding, I realized that I had to step back at some point. And guess what? The company is doing even better. It won't fall apart if you look after yourself from time to time, *mon petit*. I would rather you recognize when you need a break now, rather than when you are my age. It shouldn't take a cardiac episode to make us pay attention."

"Yes, Maman." He smiled fondly to himself. "And Esme said the same thing. That the world wouldn't end if I relaxed once in a while."

"She's right." There was a pause, then she added, "Are you spending a lot of time together?"

There was a tone of innocent speculation in her voice that sent alarm bells ringing in Stephen's head. There was absolutely no way that his mother could be matchmaking. Digging into his personal life, though? Certainly. "Not really," he answered. "We've talked a few times."

And sat at the pub. And held hands...no, not really holding hands. Not that way. And just because they shared a few long gazes and he was aware of her every time she entered a room...

Oh, no. No. Last night he'd said friends and he'd meant it. Being attracted to Esme would be a disaster in the making.

Moreover, he wouldn't hurt her for the world. And he was certain he couldn't offer her a happy ending.

He deftly changed the subject. "Maman, I also called to let you know that I have seen the plans for the garden, and I think you're going to love it. We should be able to dedicate it next spring, on Father's birthday."

"That sounds lovely. Thank you for handling this, Stephen."

"I'm the earl. I'm his son. It's not just my responsibility, it's my honor, Maman." He meant it, too—despite his conflicted feelings about his father.

Was that a sniff he heard on the other end? But Maman never let emotion get the best of her, least of all tears. Stephen felt a corresponding stinging at the back of his eyes as well.

What on earth was wrong with him? It had to be exhaustion. Perhaps the conversation this morning on top of the meeting with the solicitor had left him a tad vulnerable.

"I should go now," he said, clearing his throat for the third time that morning. "But enjoy the garden and put on your sunscreen."

She laughed then. "I will. And please send my best wishes to Mrs. Flanagan."

"I will, of course."

They said their goodbyes and Stephen hung up, then sat back in his chair. He'd nearly misted up just now, which wasn't like him at all.

Perhaps he was more stressed than he realized. It was starting to dawn on him that this break was probably long overdue. A man couldn't go on as he had been forever. But darts at the pub? There had to be a better way to unwind.

An idea popped into his head that had no place being there, involving a redhead with mossy eyes and a sweet smile.

Esme was not for him. And he needed to put her out of his mind before someone got hurt.

CHAPTER FIVE

ESME SHUT DOWN the computer in her mother's office and went off to the kitchen to find some lunch. Stephen would be looking to eat shortly.

"Hi," came his voice from behind her.

She spun around and pressed her hand to her chest. "I didn't hear you come in. I was making a list in my head."

"I thought I might get some lunch. I'm hopeful I can put together a sandwich for myself."

"Of course! I'm sure the makings are all here, including the last of the leftover roast chicken. Take a look in the fridge for what you'd like. I'll get the bread."

She retrieved a cutting board and a bread knife and then put a lovely loaf of Marjorie's harvest bread on the surface. While Stephen retrieved condiments, meat, and cheese from the fridge, she set out two plates and put the bread on each. "Butter?" she asked.

"No, thank you." He met her gaze. "I'm supposed to be making my own, remember?"

"Oh, right." She shouldn't be so flustered, but it felt different, being here alone with him now. Making a sandwich was not an intimate act and yet it felt as though it was.

She watched Stephen out of the corner of her eye, smiling a little to herself as he precisely layered on his chicken and then cut the tomato into ridiculously even slices. Not a huge surprise that he was a bit of a perfectionist, and she debated cutting a crooked slice just to see what he'd do. But he looked so pleased with himself when he finished his mammoth sandwich that she couldn't do anything but grin. She dipped a fork into the pickle jar and stabbed a thick spear, then plopped it onto his plate.

"So," she said, once they'd got themselves glasses of water and had settled at the kitchen table to eat, "what's on your agenda for the rest of the day?"

He shrugged. "Just…details. Things that would likely bore you."

"Or that I wouldn't understand?" she asked.

"Maybe, but I didn't mean it that way." His brow wrinkled.

"It's no secret I'm not a businesswoman. Though I sometimes think I'd like to be. I've kind of always dreamed of having my own little inn or B&B."

"You didn't want to go back to school?"

"I considered it. I thought I'd do business or

maybe hospitality management, since I like the industry so much. But…" She halted, then lifted her chin. "Let's just say my husband wasn't overly supportive. Of either school or me working."

Stephen's mouth dropped open as he stared at her. "What do you mean?"

"Evan's lifestyle is…well, you could probably relate more than I. He liked me to be…available, I guess is the best word. In case he needed to entertain, or if there was a company function. I was there to support his career, not the other way around."

Stephen snorted. "That's such an antiquated notion."

"Thank you! That's what I said. He didn't like it much." There were lots of things he'd criticized, too, but she wasn't about to give Stephen a laundry list of all the ways Evan had found her wanting. "But I guess your family is different. You might have grown up with that old school aristocracy and wealth thing, but you also had a strong, independent mother who ran her own business… and a massively successful one." It still blew her away when she saw the family in the tabloids or on the entertainment shows, mixing with movie stars and other celebrities.

"We did. And my father was always supportive of Maman's ambitions. I guess, at least in that way, I had strong role models."

She nodded. "And to be honest, my mum was a good role model for me. After my dad died when I was a baby, she picked herself up, found this job and made a career out of it, raising me alone."

"She's a strong woman," Stephen said.

"She is. And yet…"

She hesitated again, until Stephen leaned forward and peered into her face. "And yet what?"

"She never understood why I was unhappy with Evan. I think because she'd had to work and raise me alone, she thought I'd landed in clover when I married him. I didn't have to work, I had a gorgeous house and lovely things… I suppose, all the things she wanted for me. But" —her throat tightened— "I didn't have room to be myself, and I wasn't happy."

"Wealth and privilege can be its own cage."

"I guess you probably thought I've always been the girl in the poky flat having a pint at the pub, but I had a taste of a different life once. I didn't like it."

The air between them became awkward after those last words. She'd be a liar to say that there hadn't been a little bit of tension, even attraction on a low simmer between them the past few days. But this was the truth, though, wasn't it? Not a thing could come of it, because it wasn't just that she was of a different class. It was that she'd tried living up in that stratosphere and it wasn't for her.

* * *

Stephen's mood darkened during the rest of the day. The conversation over lunch had unsettled him, not so much from what Esme said, but what she didn't say as well. What kind of man would take a woman like Esme—gorgeous, smart, energetic—and make her into a trophy wife?

And yet…he recalled Bridget's ambitions and realized that some people aspired to that life. She'd wanted to marry an earl. She'd wanted to have the life that being the wife of the COO of Aurora could provide. A flat in Paris, country home outside London, a château in Provence. Chartered planes and champagne and designer everything. But she hadn't wanted him. It occurred to him that Bridget and this Evan guy would likely have made the perfect pair.

He'd told his mother that he needed the downtime, and it wasn't a lie, but he also needed to be…vital. What was he supposed to do, wander through the house? Watch television? Go for a stroll in the village? Two hours of that and he'd be stark raving mad. He needed to be doing something, and so he pulled up reports and started looking at proposals to expand Aurora assets into the North American market outside of New York. Several scenarios were unsustainable, especially with the current global financial market. Expansion was great but only if it worked with their overall strategy. And since one of the proposals was Bella's, it meant a difficult conversation ahead since she was the CEO.

Normally this was all in a day's work for him. But something was niggling at him. Something that he couldn't put his finger on.

He opened a drawer in the desk and pulled out a velvet box, putting it on the desk in front of him. Maybe it wasn't his job at Aurora that was causing him to be unsettled. He dealt with acquisitions, proposals, projections every day. But this... He opened the box with a slight creak of the hinge and stared at the pocket watch inside.

It had been his great-grandfather's, passed down to each earl on his twenty-fifth birthday. Twenty-five, because the story went that he'd commented to his eldest son that at twenty-one a man hadn't yet acquired a brain. Stephen remembered laughing over this with his father. By twenty-five, Stephen had his MBA and was working his way up within the company, but, as Cedric had rightfully joked, he was still clueless about women...and the kind of woman who could be a countess.

He reached out and touched the gold case, the metal cool beneath his fingertips. Being titled in this day and age was very different from his great-grandfather's time. The challenge now was stewardship of history, maintaining that history without going bankrupt.

And if Stephen had his way, the estate would

be self-sustaining, without needing any sort of infusion from Aurora's coffers.

He took the watch out of the velvet. "Why?" he whispered. "Why did you cheat on Maman? How could she take you back? How could you not acknowledge, not know, your own flesh and blood?" His jaw tightened. "How could you teach me to be a good man when you were so flawed?"

And that was just it, he realized. The memorial garden was a fine idea, he supposed. But his father was gone. Stephen was tired of being in his shadow when his actions betrayed the man he'd pretended to be. And Maman…he loved her, of course he did, but on some level, he was angry at her, too.

It was time for him to stop following in his father's footsteps, and instead start making his own path.

He lifted his head when a knock sounded at the doorjamb. "I hope I'm not disturbing you."

Esme stood in the doorway, a hesitant smile on her face. He realized he was scowling and softened his expression. "Not at all. What can I do for you?"

"Your dinner is ready," she said. "I figured you'd lost track of time."

He had. She stepped into the room as he moved to put the pocket watch back in the box. "What's that?"

He held out his hand. "It belonged to my great-grandfather. It's been passed down to every earl since."

She took it, turned the weight of it over in her hands. "It's lovely. Such a piece of history."

"I suppose it is."

"You're not fond of it?"

He sighed, taking it back from her and slipping it into the case, then tucking it in his drawer. "I am, I suppose. I've just been thinking about what it means to be the Earl of Chatsworth today. I don't know if I like the answer."

"Then change the answer," she suggested. "You are the earl. You can make of that whatever you want."

Could he, though?

"I just realized a few minutes ago that I don't want to look backward. I don't want to be the earl my father was. But I don't quite know what that means."

And Stephen was used to being on solid ground. Not knowing put him off balance, made him unsure…something he often felt but never let anyone see.

Except Esme seemed to notice everything.

She was looking at him now with a broad smile. "Congratulations," she said, her eyes lighting up. "You're about to begin what will be *your* legacy to the title. It's incredibly freeing when you finally take charge of your life and decide to make your own way…with your own boundaries."

"Like you did with your divorce?"

"Exactly," she answered. "Stephen, you can take the earldom and put your own stamp on it. You're a smart, hardworking man. You care. Those three things together mean you're going to get this right."

It was true his father had done a fine job with the actual estate. It was his personal life that he'd messed up—and covered up. Stephen's track record was nothing to celebrate, either. But he could do better now. He had no desire to marry, but if he ever did, it would be the right woman, for the right reasons. And no secrets.

Not that it was going to be an issue anyway.

"Now," she said, in her ever-cheerful voice, "I've made a chicken curry that you're going to love. Come eat and tell me your plans."

He followed her out, leaving the pocket watch—and his introspective mood—behind.

The activity of eating dinner did little to ease the ache in Esme's chest every time she got near Stephen.

She couldn't resist sneaking glimpses at his taut backside and broad shoulders. Esme was truly doomed. She was physically attracted to present-day Stephen and emotionally connected to childhood Stephen and unsure what to do with all of it. And the longer she was here, the more involved she became. She could see beneath the cool exterior and realized he was really struggling with his father's infidelity and what it all meant for him as the man stepping into the title. She thought she could understand. As a child he'd idolized his dad. Everyone had liked Cedric Pemberton and in Stephen's eyes, Cedric could do no wrong. She could only imagine what it had felt like, learning about Anemone. *Let down* didn't quite cover it.

What she really wanted to do was go to him and give him a hug. Wrap her arms around him and squeeze, as if to tell him it would be all right. The Stephen of their childhood would have welcomed it. The man before her now, with his deep frown and stiff posture, would shun such an overture of affection. Besides, just because they were talking about stuff didn't mean they were suddenly best friends again.

He was an earl. She managed a staff of six housekeepers at the local inn. He got his clothes tailor-made in Paris and London, and she popped into the chain stores on the high street to scan the sale racks. He ate at Michelin-starred restaurants, and she headed to the local where everyone knew her standing order. Moreover, these were the lives they had—for the most part—chosen.

She had no business thinking of him romantically. Especially since the last thing she would ever do is put herself in a position to be looked down upon again. To be criticized and found lacking. To be "too" anything. As she surely would be. She did not belong in his world.

And he certainly didn't belong in hers. They were eating in the kitchen again, but he looked out of place in his fine trousers, crisp shirt, and silk tie. He'd removed his suit jacket from his meeting, but that made little difference. It was in the way he carried himself, too. With breeding and confidence.

"It feels odd without the kitchen staff here," she admitted, putting down her bowl and going to fill water glasses. When she put his down in front of him, he looked up.

"Thanks."

"Of course."

She waited for him to take the first bite. This curry recipe was a particular favorite, and one she made nearly every week. When a smile broke over his face, she thought again how ridiculously handsome he was when he wasn't looking so severe.

"It's good. Really good."

"This is one of my go-tos for when I get home and I'm tired and want something I can put together easily. I try to keep things simple and nutritious."

She didn't mention that she had to work really hard not to overanalyze all her eating choices. Obsessing about what went in her mouth, feeling guilty, stepping on the scale every day…those were things she tried to keep in the past, but it was hard. Not that she'd breathe a word of it to Stephen. She'd already said too much about her marriage. Besides, his company was in fashion, for heaven's sake. Pressure to be thin and perfect had to be part of the environment, like the air that they breathed.

"What's wrong?" he asked, putting down his fork. "You've barely touched it."

"Oh! Nothing's wrong." She pasted on a smile and scooped up some basmati and chicken. "I just got lost in my thoughts for a moment."

"Anything you'd like to share?"

She looked at him and lifted an eyebrow. "Not exactly. Not unless you want to hear about my flaws, neuroses, and hang-ups."

He laughed. "I wasn't aware you had any flaws."

"We all have flaws." She rolled her eyes and took a bite of the meal.

"Sorry, I don't see any from where I'm sitting."

She looked up and met his gaze. He was watching her steadily.

"Esme, you're gorgeous. You've got the most glorious hair, and a cheeky smile and your eyes… they're full of devilment, just like they used to be. You're funny and smart." He affected his scowl again. "Evan was a damned fool."

"None of us are perfect," she whispered, touched by his words, but not quite believing him.

"Of course not. But the girl I knew was fun and

clever and had a good heart. I wish I had grown to be half as good as you."

She lifted her head sharply. "Don't say that. You're a good man."

"Am I, though?" He put down his fork. "Most people go through hard times, and they learn from it, and it makes them more understanding and compassionate. Not me. I became a bit of a git."

She snorted; she couldn't help it. "I'm guessing that's the exact term your sisters used."

He nodded. "They're right, though. Since my dad died, I've been so overwhelmed that I might have taken this 'head of the family' thing a little too much to heart. I ordered Will about when it came to dealing with Gabi…and for heaven's sake, I was going to marry her for all the wrong reasons. When it came to Charlotte, I arrived here and had a sit-down with Jacob. Charlotte was joking about pistols at dawn, but my behavior warranted it. And Anemone…" He sighed. "The circumstances weren't her fault, but I treated her horribly."

"Stephen, you ended up with a crazy amount of responsibility in a short amount of time. I'm sure you're being too hard on yourself."

"I'm not." He took a bite, chewed, swallowed, and then looked up at her again. "I was unhappy, and I took it out on those closest to me and justified it by telling myself I was looking out for them."

She didn't know what to say. She wasn't going

to argue, because it was clear that he'd done a lot of thinking today. Instead, she reached out and touched his hand with her fingers. "I'm sorry you were unhappy."

He swallowed and pulled his hand away. "It doesn't matter now. It's moving forward that matters, right?" Then he shook his head. "I think I've talked more in the last eight hours than I have in the last eight months. Sorry about that."

"Don't be." She smiled. "I'm glad you feel comfortable enough with me to share what's going on. I'm glad I can be someone for you to talk to when you need. It makes me feel…"

She broke off. She'd been going to say needed. Important. *Seen*.

And not just seen, but seen by him.

"Makes you feel what?" His voice was husky, soft, sending ripples of awareness along her nerve endings.

"Useful," she croaked, gathering up her bowl. She moved to the sink to get ready to wash the dishes.

He scooped up his last bite and then joined her at the sink, putting his hand over hers as she turned on the faucet. "Let me help with the dishes," he said quietly. "Your workday ended a while ago."

"I don't mind, really."

"If I were on my own, I'd have to do the washing up. This won't take any time at all. I'm sure

I can handle washing and drying some dishes."
He looked around, then back at her with a small
smile. "If you can show me where the towels are."

The simple request broke the tension and they
both relaxed a little, working companionably in
the quiet kitchen until the last pot was washed.
He held out his towel for her to dry her hands,
and when she reached for it, their fingers touched,
sending a jolt right to her feet at the innocent contact. Their gazes touched, held, and Esme couldn't
breathe.

Oh, no.

The moment lengthened, and her pulse ratcheted up as his gaze dropped briefly to her lips and
back up again. Not just her, then. He was feeling it, too. This pull that happened at the oddest
times, taking them from old friends to something
new and exciting…something that could never be,

Despite all her self-assurances about not wanting to be a part of his kind of life, she did want
him. And right now he was leaning closer, closer…

The sound of the *Bridgerton* theme blared
through the kitchen: Esme's mobile. As her cheeks
flushed, she stepped away and hurried to the
counter, where she'd left it charging. She answered
while Stephen calmly folded the dish towel, and
she wondered how he could be so damned calm
when she was struggling to breathe normally and
answer the phone as if nothing had happened.

"Hello, Mum."

Stephen's gaze slid to hers again, concern in the dark depths, and she liked him all the more for it. Esme gave a nearly imperceptible shake of her head—nothing was wrong—and so he went about looking in cabinets and cupboards to put things away. When she hung up a few moments later, he stopped what he was doing and faced her. "Everything all right?"

She nodded. "Mum just asked if I could pick up her new anti-nausea medication on the way home. The chemo plays havoc with her tummy." She pushed down the worry—these were expected side effects, after all—and tried a smile. "Would it be all right if I took some of the leftover curry? If she's not feeling well, she probably didn't make any dinner."

"Of course you can, don't be silly." He turned in a circle, then faced her again and held out his hands. "I would get you a dish to put it in, but I have no idea where anything is."

She laughed a little, trying to get them back to a "normal" vibe...whatever that was. "They're in here." She went to a cabinet where a selection of covered dishes was organized precisely by size.

She went to the counter where the larger dish was cooling and scooped some out. "Is there anything you need before I go?" she asked, and chanced a look up at him. If he mentioned the almost-kiss, she was sure she'd die of both embarrassment and want. But he shook his head, obviously recovering better than she was able to as he acted as if nothing had happened.

"Go look after your mum and tell her I said hello and to follow doctor's orders," he said softly.

It was easier to dismiss him when his voice was hard and impatient, like it had been when he first arrived. But these moments, when the caring man beneath the hard exterior shone through? In these moments, he was hard to resist. If he took two steps toward her and gave her any encouragement at all, she rather suspected she'd find herself in his arms.

How was it possible to want something so much and be so afraid of it at the same time?

"I will." She took a step back and inhaled deeply. His words about following doctor's orders prompted the fear that she tried to prevent taking over, but sometimes the thoughts snuck in. Her mum was her only family. What if she lost her, too?

"What is it?" Stephen asked.

"It's nothing. I just worry about her. About... losing her."

Understanding warmed his eyes and his mouth. "Of course you do. I wish I could offer you guarantees."

"No one can," she replied, her voice shaking a little.

"But your mum is a strong woman, and she's getting good care, yes?" His gaze sharpened.

"Esme, if anything's been lacking, please tell me. If there's anything I can do to help…"

"No! I mean, she's had very good care, the best. And the family has already been so generous and understanding. I'm sorry I said anything. I try not to bring my personal problems to work."

"But we're friends, too, aren't we?" He stepped closer, his gaze never leaving hers.

"I suppose," she answered, biting down on her lip. Complicated friends.

His gaze followed the action and her breath caught. It was torture when he looked at her lips that way, as if he wanted to kiss them, taste them…

She stepped back, knowing she couldn't allow herself to get sucked into whatever silly attraction she was feeling. Hadn't he just said *friends*? Being foolish would only break the tentative relationship they'd forged over the past few days.

"I—I should get going. I'll see you in the morning." Because she still had to be here to do her job, even though the rest of the staff was gone, and she was in this house with him, *alone*.

He stayed where he was, thankfully, and she turned to head toward the kitchen door.

"Es?"

He used the shortened version of her name again, and oh, the memories that single syllable brought back. It stopped her in her tracks and made her turn, though she was now several feet away from him.

"You will let me know if there's anything I can do for Mrs. F, won't you?" he asked.

She nodded, too touched at his caring tone to risk answering. And then she turned around and got out of there as fast as she could without running.

Stephen Pemberton might think himself a git and think he'd let down his family, but all she could see was the concern in his eyes and the flash of vulnerability anytime he spoke of his family and his recent actions. He was a good man who had suffered his own pain, a man who appeared strong and formidable but had a heart that could easily be wounded. It had always been so, but perhaps no one got to see that side of him. Perhaps he took great care to keep it hidden.

But she knew. And because she knew, she also knew she was in grave danger of getting in over her head.

CHAPTER SIX

MARY FLANAGAN WAS too determined to let anything get her down for long, which was why Esme
was so shocked to find her mum sitting in a chair
with her feet up and a blanket over her lap. Esme
covered her alarm and pasted on a smile. "Hello,
Mum."

"Hello, darling."

"Feeling all right, then?" Esme went to the
kitchen and automatically filled a glass with some
water and took it to her mother's side.

"Tired today. And a little cold, though I don't
know why."

Esme peered into her face. "Chills?"

Mary flapped a hand. "Don't fuss. I'm fine."

"I'm going to take your temperature just in
case." The chemo meant that Mary was particularly susceptible to infections. If she were running
a fever, she should see a doctor.

She grabbed the digital thermometer and took
a reading from her mum's ear. Her temperature
was slightly elevated, which gave Esme some con-

cern. "We'll call the doctor in the morning," she advised. "And I'm staying here tonight to keep an eye on you."

"Oh, for heaven's sake—"

"I don't want to hear it. Have you eaten any dinner?"

Mary's mouth took on a stubborn set.

"I figured as much. I brought you some curry." She put the thermometer away and headed toward the small kitchen. "Stubborn old cow," she muttered.

There was a bark of laughter from behind her and a sharp, "I heard that, brat."

Esme smiled. Their banter was a form of affection between them, and when her mum talked back Esme knew nothing was super serious. Still, she didn't want to take any chances. "Drink your water and I'll heat this up in a jiffy," she called.

She put the dish in the microwave and started tea. Before long it was all heated up, the tea was steeping, and she carried the simple meal to her mum on a tray.

"Oh, Esme. You didn't have to go to that bother."

Esme put down the tray. "Leftover curry is hardly a bother. Tomorrow I'll make sure you have something, too. You just tell me what seems appetizing, and I'll see to it."

"Thank you. And for picking up my medication." There was always a period of nausea and vomiting after a round of chemo, and ensuring Mary got nutrition during those days was a challenge.

"I'll be back with the tea."

She poured them each a cup and took it to the living room, placing her mum's on her tray but holding hers in her hand as she sat on the edge of the sofa. She sipped her tea and let her mother eat, all the while thinking about Stephen's parting words. His offer to help was sweet. More so because she knew he'd been absolutely sincere.

"You're quiet, Es."

She looked up. "Oh, just stuck in my thoughts, I guess."

"How are things going with Stephen?"

She hadn't told her mum that she was the only household staff working right now, and that she and Stephen were alone in the house. For some reason, she wanted to keep that knowledge to herself, even though it was hardly a secret. But her mum would ask questions—questions Esme didn't want to answer.

"Fine," she answered, making her voice bright. "He's overseeing the plans for the memorial garden. I believe they're breaking ground tomorrow."

Mary nodded. "It's a lovely idea. Cedric was a good man."

Esme had always thought so, too, but the news of Anemone's parentage had changed her view of the man who'd been a part of their lives for so long. "It's been hard on Stephen since his father's death," she said. "And finding out about his half-sister. Those kids worshiped their father. News like that is a blow."

"Surprised me, too," Mary mused. "But people make mistakes. The worst thing we can ever do is expect someone to be perfect, and then act surprised when they're not."

When her mum said things like that she often wondered if it was just her folksy wisdom or if there was a little dig about Esme's marriage to Evan hidden in the words. Mary had liked Evan a lot, but she hadn't had to live with him. Certainly hadn't had to deal with his nitpicking and putdowns.

"It does set people up for failure, doesn't it?" Esme asked, her voice a little pointed. For all her mum's talk, Esme had always rather felt like she never quite measured up to her mum's expectations.

They loved each other dearly. But their relationship, like any other mother-daughter relationship, had its foibles. "Anyway, Stephen is well."

Mary smiled. "You spent a lot of time together as children."

"Until it got to be too inappropriate."

Mary nodded. "Well, yes. He went away to school, after all. But until then, you were like peas in a pod." She scooped up a spoonful of curry and popped it into her mouth.

"I'm not sure anyone realized how much I missed him after he was gone." Esme met her mum's gaze. "He was my best friend. And the girls at school…"

Mary's eyes softened. "I know, darling. Those years are always awkward…"

"But up until then I had Stephen after school. We did homework together. Climbed trees."

"Got into trouble," Mary added, chuckling. "And don't tell me it was all Stephen's fault. He covered for you."

Esme grinned. "A time or two." She hesitated and then added, "It's been good to see him, though. We've had a few laughs about those years."

Mary Flanagan had always been close with her employers, but her gaze sharpened now, and Esme felt as if her mum could see right past the deliberate "catching up" vibe she was projecting and into her heart, which was a lot more attached.

"As long as there's nothing improper," Mary cautioned.

"Give me some credit, Mum." Esme took a sip of tea. "We were childhood friends. But he's the Earl of Chatsworth, and what am I? I know better."

Mary put down her knife and fork. "That is not what I meant, Esme. You're just as good as any of the Pembertons, and just you mind that."

Esme stared.

"It's got nothing to do with good people. Heavens, having money and a title doesn't make someone virtuous. If only. And I'm not saying the Pembertons aren't good people. They are. Some of the finest I've ever met. Maybe improper was the wrong word. It's just that you work for him right now. What's that line from the movie we watch all the time?"

Esme knew exactly what she was referring to. "Don't dip your nib in the office ink."

Mary chuckled. "That's the one." Her green gaze held Esme's. "The Pembertons live in a very different world, pet. People like us…we don't belong there."

A part of Esme wanted to dispute it. It was a classist statement and she wanted to say that the "people like us" could belong wherever they wanted. But she also understood what her mum was saying. After all, Evan had been upper-class and that had been a disaster. She was tempted to remind her mum of that fact but didn't want to get into the subject of her failed marriage.

Besides, if she flipped it around, she could just as easily say that Stephen didn't belong in a world like hers. The physical attraction she felt was nothing more than an inconvenience and the result of a romantic and sexual dry spell. And it was a stupid thing to be thinking about, anyway. Nothing had happened with Stephen. Nothing *would* happen with Stephen.

"Nothing to fear there, Mum. It's been a fun little trip down memory lane, but that's all there is to it. Besides, I quite like the life I've built for myself here. I have a job I like. Friends. You're here. I have my own little flat... I'm contented. And before you say it, yes, it sucks to be single at thirty-four, but better that than be with the wrong person, which I was." She lifted her chin. "And while I've enjoyed this little conversational detour, we really should be talking about how you're feeling. Better since having something to eat?"

"Fine as a flea," Mary said, making her laugh. "But I know you're going to stay, anyway, so let's break out a movie and make a night of it."

Esme was glad her mum wasn't going to make a big time about her staying over. She found a movie for them to watch and then pulled out her phone to send a quick message.

Mum's a little under the weather. Spending the night so I can call the doctor in the morning. Will you be all right for breakfast?

It wasn't long and a reply came back.

Of course! I'll be fine. Let me know if you need anything.

She put the phone away, thinking about how kind and generous Stephen was, when everyone thought he was stern and formidable and...cold.

He was anything but. And maybe she was the only one who knew it. That, more than anything else, made him so very dangerous to her heart.

Stephen was in the kitchen making coffee when Esme came in, her black uniform replaced by faded jeans and a cute, flowered top in light blue. With her coppery hair tumbling over her shoulders, she took his breath away.

"Good morning," he said, and she smiled at him, sending a warmth straight into his heart. She was like a ray of sunshine.

"Good morning to you, too. You made out okay with breakfast?"

"Just fine. I need another caffeine infusion, though."

She went to the cupboard to get a second mug; apparently she was joining him. "I see you left your suit in your closet. Denim suits you."

He'd put on a pair of jeans and a short-sleeved button-down, and it felt strange but also comfortable. "We have an agreement," he reminded her.

"Indeed. Do you have enough water in the press for two cups?"

"I do. How's your mum?"

Esme went to the fridge for milk. "I just took her home from the doctor's. Her fever was still up a little this morning. He's not overly worried. It could be nothing, but it's worth watching. Besides, if she gets sick, she might have to delay her next chemo treatment. So I'll be keeping an eye on her, looking for any additional symptoms. Her test results will be back later."

"I'm sorry, but glad you were able to go with her."

"Thank you for that. Mum tends to downplay things, but she can't get away with that if I go with her."

Stephen smiled. Esme and Mrs. F were clearly still very close. He was glad of it. Esme stood beside him as he poured, and the light fragrance of her perfume wrapped around him, fresh and floral and clean. His jaw tightened and he stirred the sugar into his coffee a little aggressively. He thought about Esme far too often. He thought about her gorgeous hair and her sparkling eyes and wide smile. The touch of her cool fingers on his hand, the sound of her laugh.

At first it had been memories of their childhoods together, rainy days in the library, hot chocolate in the kitchen, summer days at the pond or climbing trees in the orchard. But he'd be a big fat liar if he didn't admit—at least to himself—that he was attracted to Esme for the woman she was now. Kind. Independent. Forgiving.

Which was completely impossible. Wasn't it?

Why did it matter that they came from different economic situations? He didn't give a damn about that kind of thing.

He stood there, his coffee growing cold, and stared at Esme for several moments.

"Are you okay?" she asked, lifting her cup to sip. "You seem out of sorts." Then she waited patiently for him to answer, as if sensing he was trying to sort it out. How was it she knew that about him so easily?

"Yes, I'm fine." The response came out sharpish, and he sighed. "Sorry. I didn't mean to snap."

"I don't care about that. But I'm concerned about you, Stephen. About why you're so tightly wound. Oh, you forget now and again and loosen up, but you're still..." She sighed. "You're unhappy. I can tell. You used to get the same look on your face when you were frustrated at something."

He ran his hand over his face. "I think it just takes practice to let things go. And it's something I haven't had much practice at...ever." He stopped, unsure how to articulate what he was feeling. "Yesterday I was all set to carve out my own path. Today... I have no idea what that looks like."

Esme came forward and put her hand on his arm. "As my nan used to say, you're all sixes and sevens. But you'll figure it out. Don't be so hard on yourself, and give it time."

He nodded, all too aware of her fingers on his arm, how cool and soft and reassuring they were.

And he wanted to talk to her about the bubble of discontent that had been sitting on his chest for so long, but it was hard. Of all the people in the world, he should be able to trust Esme, but trusting was difficult. He'd thought he could trust lots of people before and look where that had got him.

A broken engagement.

Left at the altar.

She took a step back. "You should finish your coffee. Didn't you say the team was breaking ground today?"

He nodded and reached for his cup. "They are. Scheduled to be here in about an hour. Esme, I—" But he stopped, not knowing what to say next.

She let out a sigh and smiled. "It's okay. Stephen, you've always been one to hold your emotions inside. You're a man of action instead. I know talking about your feelings is probably way down on your list of desired activities, and that's okay. I just know that you're struggling. You need to find a way to put down the burden you're carrying, and then sort out what parts of it you're willing to pick up again." Her green eyes were soft with compassion. "And I know because I've been there. So if you need a friend, I'm here. Your secrets are as safe with me as they always were, I promise."

She had no idea that part of his problem was her...or at least the attraction that kept getting in the way every time they were in a room together.

What scared him the most was that he did want to open up and let her in, tell her everything. He wanted to pull her into his arms and hold on, and last night... God, last night he'd taken one look at her soft, pink lips and wanted to kiss the daylights out of her. Out of Esme, the girl who'd once dared him to eat a worm. The girl who had angrily cried the day he told her he was going away to school and how he was going to be a great earl like his father and be rich and powerful. That girl had said hurtful things and then affected a perfect, deep curtsy before spitting the words, "Goodbye, my lord," in his direction, a mockery of everything he'd thought was important.

He'd hurt her. And to indulge in this little fantasy of them being together would hurt her in the end, so he shoved his feelings down with all his other ones and locked them away.

"I'm fine, but I appreciate the offer." He knew his tone was back to being cool again, saw the rebuff in her eyes as hurt crossed her face. She was right. He did have a hard time letting go, and he didn't know how to stop hurting people because of it.

"I'd better get to work," she said softly. "Before my boss finds out I've been slacking in the kitchen."

He appreciated her attempt at lightening the mood, but it was spoiled, nonetheless. She slid past him and out the door, presumably to her office to start her day, or at least away from him. Stephen sighed, took a drink of his cooling coffee, and forced himself to swallow. As far as secrets, she didn't know the half of it. And sharing his vulnerabilities had never gotten him anywhere.

CHAPTER SEVEN

ESME RESTED HER head on her hand and let out a long, slow breath.

It was a blessing and a curse, her tender heart. It made her empathetic—a good quality, surely—but it also meant she sometimes took on more than she needed to when it came to other people's struggles. First her mum, and now Stephen.

It was more than that with Stephen, though. The wounded boy in him called to her heart. But the man he'd become…she responded to him like a woman. Last night sleep had been a long time coming because she'd been imagining what it might have been like had her mum not phoned and they'd actually kissed.

Not that she'd admit it to anyone other than herself, but she couldn't stop thinking about Stephen as a lover. And every time she put on that bright smile and pretended to be perky and friendly and helpful, it cost her just a little bit.

This morning it had taken all she had not to go over to him and put her arms around him. But then what would have happened? She was sure he didn't feel the same way about her, even if he was feeling the tiniest bit of attraction. Not once since he'd arrived home had he even suggested he was interested in her in that way. They were friends, and he made sure to repeat it at regular intervals. Sure, he cared, but that wasn't the same thing. He cared about his sisters, too, and his horses, and probably puppies and kittens.

Besides, her tender heart had got her into tons of trouble before. She had a disturbing tendency to look for the best in people and then ended up disappointed.

She let out a little growl and decided to check on the progress in the garden. The sound of heavy equipment had filtered through to her little office and she'd found herself curious as to what was being dug up. The fact that Stephen was probably watching didn't matter; she could stay out of sight and at least get an idea of how it would all take shape. All she knew right now was that the area just above a little copse of trees was going to become the memorial garden, and that the current rose garden would lead to its entrance.

She grabbed her sunglasses and headed outside. The day was another sunny one, though showers were likely to sweep through later in the evening. The rose garden was past its prime now, with only a few straggling blooms giving a wisp of sweet scent, but Esme took her time walking the stone path past the different varieties. The noise from the equipment ground through the air, so foreign to her ears when the estate was generally so quiet and peaceful.

At the edge of the rose garden, she stopped and stared at the chaos before her.

There was a reason they called it "breaking ground." A large backhoe was scooping up dirt and putting it in a huge pile, while stakes outlined the perimeter of the proposed garden. It was a large space, but other than that, there was no clear clue as to what the finished installation would look like. A few workmen stood to the side, pointing and talking while the equipment operator went on digging, digging.

Digging into the green space where Esme and Stephen had once run free, heading for the grove of ash and beech trees. Stephen had wanted to build a treehouse, but Cedric had said no. Instead, the two of them had cobbled together a fort on the ground. Esme had taken out a large plastic storage tub, which held a couple of old cushions and a blanket so they had something to sit on and Stephen had been in charge of snacks, since he could always sweet-talk Marjorie into something delicious after school. There had always been lots of biscuits and a bottle of something to drink that they'd shared.

It had been such a good childhood, until he'd been sent away.

She could still see the shady trees and wondered why she hadn't yet wandered through the field to visit their old haunts. Probably because she'd only come back to work, not play, and to indulge in a walk down memory lane meant she wasn't doing her job—the job that was her mum's livelihood and life. Ever since coming to the manor, Esme felt such pressure to do everything right, as her mum would.

It dawned on her that Stephen must feel the same way about his title, only magnified by about a hundred. After all, he'd been training for this moment since before his voice had even changed.

He wasn't anywhere to be found at the moment, and the pull to the grove was strong. It wouldn't hurt to take a peek, would it? See if that fort was still there somehow? She doubted it, but she wanted to see anyway. Wanted to go back to those idyllic days before she'd found herself without her best friend, before she'd gone on to school without him, teased by girls and boys alike, before she'd found herself growing breasts and getting curves and attracting unwanted attention. Her stomach clenched, but she let out a deep breath. She'd hated her teen years.

She skirted the construction zone and waded through the grass toward the wilder parts of the property—the grove and the field beyond that was bisected by a brook. The summer air was fragrant with the scent of grass and flowers and the redolent aroma of warm and fertile earth. Esme breathed deeply, soaking it all in, heading for the trees and the shade she would find within.

The path was still there, which surprised her. Perhaps a bit narrower than it had been, but there nonetheless, leading into the leafy canopy of beech and ash. The tension Esme had felt in her muscles earlier eased; her breath came out in a glorious sigh. Being here was a happy place. Why hadn't she come before?

The fort would be just around the bend in the path, if she remembered correctly. Her stride quickened as she got closer, hoping it was still standing though it was doubtful after over twenty years. A few more steps…

She halted, shocked at the scene before her.

It was as if nothing had changed at all! A closer glance showed her the exact opposite of what she'd expected had happened. It hadn't fallen into disrepair, hadn't been blown down during a winter gale. It had been reinforced. Perhaps made a little bigger. Someone was still using this fort.

She stepped forward carefully, curious. A branch snapped under her feet, the sound sharp in the quiet. Even the birds had gone surprisingly silent. Esme bit down on her lip and took another two steps closer to the opening that was the door.

"I brought the biscuits. Do you have anything to sit on?"

She gasped and pressed a hand to her heart

at the sound. "Stephen! What on earth are you doing here?"

He poked his head out so she could see him, a small smile on his face. "I could ask you the same thing."

He was here. In their fort. They were in their mid-thirties, for heaven's sake. "I was wondering if this still existed. Clearly it does." She waved a finger at the structure. "Is this you? I mean...did you do all this?"

He nodded. "I did. Came back on summer hols one year and fixed it up. Whenever I wanted to disappear, it was here for me. You'd think there'd be lots of room at the house to find privacy. Not so much, as it happens. But some of Marjorie's biscuits and a book did the trick. When I got older, I'd grab a Pimm's and hide out."

He leaned back so she couldn't see him anymore. "Are you coming in?"

She shouldn't. Heavens. The two of them sitting in some tree fort like children...but excitement rushed through her veins. How many people got a chance to recapture their childhood? "What kind of biscuits are we talking about?"

He laughed, and she delighted in the rare sound. "Hobnobs, of course. I found them in a tin in the kitchen this morning."

She went to the opening and looked inside. There was an old plaid blanket on the ground, and Stephen sat there with his long legs crossed.

He swept his arm wide, inviting her in, and his sleeve rode up his arm a little, revealing a partial tattoo. She blinked. The Earl of Chatsworth—the uptight, autocratic eldest child of this blue-blooded family—had a tat. Nothing could have surprised her more.

She wondered if they should compare. The thought of showing him the tattoo just above her tailbone sent heat rushing to her cheeks, so she dipped her head and stepped inside the structure.

She sat down immediately; the fort was far too short for either of them to stand. Stephen's grin widened, transforming his face, and he held out the tin as she crossed her legs. "Biscuit?"

She reached in, took a Hobnob, and nibbled on the edge. So delicious. A few crumbs landed on her shirt, and she brushed them off. "I haven't been here since you left years ago. There wasn't any reason for me to visit the manor much, and when I did, I...well, I didn't have the same liberties. I ended up staying in the kitchen or in Mum's office. I certainly wasn't in a position to have run of the place."

"But you've been back here for weeks now." Stephen reached for another cookie. "Why wait until today?"

She shrugged, trying to rid herself of the surreal feeling of being in a childhood fort with him after all these years. "I went to see the garden site. Then I saw the grove, and, well, curiosity got the best of me." She finished her cookie and looked up at him. "When the entire household staff was on, I couldn't just disappear. My mum…well, those are big shoes to fill. Especially as her daughter. I think everyone expects me to do things exactly the same way."

"But you don't?"

"No one does. Your father was the earl, and so are you, but there are differences between you. You probably feel pressured to carry on the same legacy, but you shouldn't. You should be able to make your own."

He stared at her for a long moment. "Not a single person has understood that in the last two years," he said quietly. "The great Cedric Pemberton. And now the scandalous Cedric Pemberton. To be honest, I don't think I'll ever be as great as he was. And I certainly don't want to be—" He halted.

"His infidelity has left its mark. Of course it has." She stated it plainly. Stephen wasn't the kind of man who beat around the bush or prevaricated. "He made a mistake, Stephen. A big one, for sure, but he was human. It doesn't mean he wasn't a good father to you."

"It does mean he wasn't a good father to Anemone, though," Stephen added. "And I feel guilty about that."

"The guilt isn't yours. And have you said that to Anemone?"

He didn't answer, just reached for another biscuit. Esme smiled to herself. Stephen was so proud. She could imagine admitting such a thing would be difficult for him.

"And what happened with you, Stephen?" She picked up the lid of the tin and put it back on so neither of them could hide behind the sweet treats. "Your broken engagement. The wedding that wasn't."

He brushed his hands together. "I should probably get back."

He went to move but she grabbed his arm. "Not this time. Don't shut me out. Not talking about it isn't going to make it go away, you know." She paused before deciding to dive in. "What happened with Bridget? If you loved her, why did you break it off?" She knew from her mum that Stephen had done the breaking up.

He sat back down. "She wasn't who I thought she was. She..." He frowned, and his jaw took on a resolute set. "She was far more interested in what I could provide than in being with me. And maybe I should have expected it, but when I looked at my parents, who loved each other so much..." He stopped, then looked up at Esme. "Which sounds like a joke, right? Because how could someone love his wife so much and have an affair with someone else?"

Her heart went out to him. She'd never had to worry about her father falling off his pedestal;

he'd never been up there to begin with. Her dad had died when she was little; she didn't even remember him. It was different for Stephen. He'd idolized his dad.

"Maybe I just expect too much from people," he said roughly.

"No, you don't." Esme scooted over a little, so she was sitting closer to him, and put her hand on his knee. "Stephen, expecting someone to honor their promises and expecting someone to love you for you and not your money and title is the *bare minimum*. But your faith has been shattered, and so now you don't trust anyone to keep their word. Am I close?"

His dark eyes held hers. "Closer than I'm comfortable with. But then, you've always been able to read me."

"Is there anyone you do trust? Because that's a pretty lonely place to be."

Stephen put his hand over hers, which was still on his knee. The grip was warm, firm, and encompassed her entire hand.

"I trust you, Esme. You've never let me down."

And then he leaned forward and touched his lips to hers.

Stephen wasn't sure what had prompted him to move that little bit forward and kiss her, but he couldn't find it in himself to regret it…not when she tasted so sweet.

Her breath came out in a sigh as she lifted her hand and cupped it softly around the curve of his neck. My God, this was Esme he was kissing. The girl he'd played with, skinned knees with, helped with history homework while she'd helped him with math.

But she wasn't that girl any longer. She was a woman—a beautiful, compassionate, alluring woman—and he'd been thinking about doing just this for three days.

He reached out and circled her waist with his hands, then pulled her onto his lap. The movement caused their mouths to break apart, and her startled emerald eyes met his, her lips plumped from kissing. "Stephen, I—"

He gave his head a small shake, halting her words, and then kissed her again, as if he couldn't possibly get enough of her to quench his thirst.

She pressed closer to him, welcoming his nearness, and he stopped thinking about everything except her—the feel and taste of her. She swamped his senses and he succumbed willingly, nipping at her lips, running his hand down her rib cage.

Another shift—hers, this time—and she'd straddled him, cupped his face in her hands, and had taken over.

Nothing could have surprised and pleased him more. He cupped his hands on her bottom and held her close. The desire to make love to her here was overwhelming. No one would find them. He imagined her fiery hair strewn over the rough wool blanket, her creamy skin, open to the air and his gaze…

He moved his hand over her breast and felt the tip with his thumb. Esme. This was his Esme. The need to truly make her his roared through his veins.

But he couldn't. It took all his willpower to put his hands on her arms and break the kisses that consumed them both, but he did it. "Esme. We can't. My God. I'm so sorry. I shouldn't have…" He didn't know what to say. Both of them were breathing hard.

But what surprised him most was when he looked in her eyes and saw them swimming with tears.

"Esme…what…?"

"It's okay. I shouldn't have either… I was foolish to think…" She scrambled off his lap, and he immediately felt the loss of her. He wanted her close again.

"Foolish to think what? That I could want you?"

She didn't answer, but the pink that climbed her cheeks and the way she avoided his gaze answered the question anyway.

How the hell could she think she was anything less than desirable? He reached out and put his hand along her face.

"I wasn't planning to kiss you. It was an impulse, but the spark…oh, there's more than a spark, there. Esme. Look at me."

She obeyed, her cheeks reddening further.

"I didn't expect it to be that hot. That instant. And I stopped because I don't have protection and if we'd kept going, that was where we would end up. With that choice to make."

She swallowed. "I practically jumped on you."

"Only because you beat me to it. I mean, I understand that it's weird. We're…friends. Though if I'm honest…"

He trailed off, thinking back to those days when he'd turned thirteen and she'd been twelve and sometimes the atmosphere between them had got awkward. Her breasts had just been budding but he'd noticed. And sometimes if they touched carelessly, he'd reacted in a new, exciting and frankly, uncomfortable way.

"If you're being honest, what?"

He lifted a shoulder and smiled at her a little. "If I hadn't gone away to school, things would have changed between us anyway. It was already starting to get awkward."

Her mouth dropped open. "For you, too?"

He nodded. "Maybe we shouldn't be so surprised that there's…chemistry."

He'd thought that the admission might ease something between them, but instead Esme seemed to pull away. Had he said something wrong?

"I should go back up to the house," she said, rising to her knees.

"Esme, wait. Don't go. If we don't talk about this it's going to be awkward. Please."

She hesitated.

"You pulled away when I said we had chemistry. Please tell me why."

She let out a long sigh. "This is a mistake. Thinking we were friends…we both know this can't go anywhere, and you're not just some random guy."

He held her gaze. "You mean I could hurt you."

She nodded slowly. "And it makes me feel very vulnerable to admit that."

She really had no idea that she also had the power to hurt him.

"We *are* friends," he asserted. He didn't care about their differences or that years had passed. "And I don't have many."

She snorted. "That's ridiculous. Look at you."

Annoyance flared at her careless words. "Why is it ridiculous? I have very few people in my life that I trust. That I feel aren't working some sort of angle because of who I am. You… I've known you since I was a child. I not only know you're not working an angle, I also think that my money and title actually put me at a disadvantage. I get the idea that this is not a life you'd want."

She looked at him steadily, then finally replied. "If that is the case, and it isn't what I want, then why would I sleep with you? It isn't something I do casually, Stephen. And especially not with people I value as friends. Why would I want to mess that up?"

"You tell me." He was unable to hold back his frustration. "You were the one on my lap."

She scrambled to her feet and out the door of the fort.

"Esme, wait. I didn't really mean that." He followed her out, straightening his shirt as he went.

She turned toward him.

"But you did. And we both know nothing can come of this. I'd be a liar to say I'm not attracted. That kissing you wasn't…" She huffed out a huge breath. "It was really good, okay? And hell yes, I've wondered what it would be like. But if we did more than that, we'd stop being friends. Or feelings would get involved and one of us would end up hurt." She took a few steps backward. "I'm not up for that, Stephen. I'm just not. Not again."

She turned and walked away, her feet crunching against twigs and stones leading to the path.

Stephen ran a hand through his hair, watched her go. She was right, of course. But what had she meant by "again?" If she meant her ex-husband, he really wanted to punch that guy in the face.

"I'm an idiot. Just a complete idiot."

Esme sat across from her best friend, Phoebe, and stared into her glass of beer. The whole afternoon she'd been playing the scene in the fort over and over in her mind until it nearly drove her mad. And this was not something she could talk over with her mum. There was no doubt that Mary Flanagan would have a lot to say about Esme letting personal feelings get in the way of work. Esme was in no mood for a lecture.

"You're not an idiot," Phoebe said, picking up her G&T and taking a sip. Phoebe arched a dark eyebrow as she stared at Esme. "I've seen pics of him in the tabloids. He's scrummy."

Esme snorted. Stephen would hate being described as *scrummy*. She caught Phoebe's smile and returned it, though rather reluctantly. Phoebe flipped her dark brown hair over her shoulder and lifted her chin in triumph. "You know you think so. I bet he smells good, too."

Oh, he did. The Aurora cosmetics department had a number of lovely scents, and Stephen smelled so delicious, like sandalwood and cedar and something clean and crisp. Particularly in the hollow of his neck, as the summer warmth amplified the intensity of the fragrance. He'd said he'd only stopped because he didn't have protection… he'd wanted to have sex with her. She still couldn't quite wrap her head around that.

"Look," Phoebe said, gesturing with the straw from her glass. "Your ex, who shall not be named, was an arse. We both know it. You cannot judge the Earl of Chatsworth by that crappy yardstick."

"I know that, intellectually," Esme retorted, poking her fork into the salad she'd ordered. "In practice it's a very different thing. And even if it weren't, as you say, he's the earl." Phoebe opened her mouth to say something, and Esme held up a hand, halting her. "That is not the life for me, and we both know it. Can you see me at one of their parties? Pheebs, I'm the woman who serves the canapes, not eats them."

"Canapes are overrated. And if you were Stephen Pemberton's wife, you could eat whatever you wanted."

"Wife? Okay, now you have lost the plot." Esme laughed, even as something wistful twisted inside her gut. Today, sitting in the fort together, kissing, touching him…for a brief moment it hadn't mattered that he was rich as Croesus and as handsome as the devil. He'd just been the person who *got* her like no one else ever had.

Phoebe took a bite of her dinner and then started gesturing with her fork, looking like she was conducting an invisible orchestra. "If I hear you say that you're not good enough for him, I'm going to have to stage an intervention."

"It's not even that." It was, a bit, but not in the way Phoebe was thinking. "Look, I know what the ex who shall not be named did. He chipped away at my self-esteem and made me doubt myself, and yeah, sometimes I have to really work to break out of those patterns. But it's not just his behavior that concerns me. It's my own. Why would I put myself in a position where I stood a very good chance of feeling overlooked and invisible? I've had to really work at overcoming that already. I can't put myself in a situation that risks me repeating that behavior. I've fought so hard to have my own life, my own agency. I'm so scared to lose myself again."

Phoebe's smile fell from her lips and she put down her fork. "Damn, Es. I can't actually argue with that. That's really self-aware of you."

"Stephen's a good man. He wouldn't mean to. But it's not about him. It's about me, and how I respond to things. It feels as if I'd be setting myself up for failure. I had messages for years about how I wasn't a good wife, how I needed to lose a stone or two, how I wasn't intellectually his equal. It would be very easy to go down that road again with a family as powerful as the Pembertons, especially considering the industry they're in." She let out a sigh. "Walking away from my marriage was the best thing I ever did, but I didn't do it without scars."

"I'd like to give him some scars," Phoebe muttered darkly, and Esme laughed.

She picked at her salad while Phoebe scarfed down her chicken alfredo.

"But Pheebs?"

"Yes, darling?"

"How do I go back to work there again? With

it just being the two of us? How do I not jump his bones again? Because it was really, really good."

Phoebe burst out laughing, while Esme stared dolefully at her dinner. She started to push her plate away when Phoebe put her hand on Esme's wrist, halting the movement.

"You can't have any pudding unless you finish your meat," she said in an exaggerated voice, imitating Pink Floyd.

Esme shook her head and chuckled. "This is why you're my best friend. You are so totally random and wonderful."

"Of course I am. And so the advice I'm going to give you this evening—aren't you the lucky one—is threefold. One, stop worrying so much about one kiss from a guy who is only going to be in town for another week or two. You managed to go twenty years without crossing paths, and you wouldn't be now, either, except you're covering for your mum. Two, you could stand to have a bit of a fling, since by this time I'm a little concerned about the neglect your girly parts have suffered. This hasn't been just a dry spell, it's been the freaking desert."

Esme's cheeks heated, and she hoped no one at any of the nearby tables could hear Pheebs's life advice.

"Three," Phoebe said, ticking it off on her fingers, "you cannot leave this evening without getting whatever makes up the Death by Chocolate on the dessert menu. We can share."

As Esme dutifully ate her vegetables, she considered Phoebe's advice. It was true she hadn't been with anyone in a very long time. In fact, she'd only had sex once since her divorce, after she'd been out on exactly three dates with someone she met on a dating app, and she'd known immediately that it had been a mistake. She wasn't made for casual sex, couldn't shrug it off as simply a nice evening or attending to her needs. Both of those were true and perfectly fine, but the problem was it had left her feeling emptier rather than fulfilled...beyond the obvious, that was.

She supposed now that it was good the ex—she and Phoebe had a pact to not call him by name—was not her last. Not just because of how long it had been but because he'd always found her lacking in some way. At least Mr. Third Date had been...pleasurable.

But not fireworks. The whole thing hadn't been as incendiary as five minutes in Stephen's arms with all their clothes on.

She reached for her beer and took a long drink. Had the pub just got hotter? Or maybe it was her mind automatically straying to the thought of Stephen and fireworks and wondering what it would be like to have all that intensity focused on her.

But what was the point? With Stephen—if he

even wanted to—it would still be casual because a relationship was out of the question.

And maybe if she kept saying it to herself, she'd believe it.

The chocolate torte came, complete with a scoop of ice cream and hot fudge sauce. Esme considered saying no, thinking of the extra few pounds she always felt she carried around, and then took a breath and pushed out the thought, replacing it with healthier ones. She was fine just the way she was. And she could surely share a dessert with her best friend on their weekly dinner dates.

When they'd finished the meal with the torte and coffee, Phoebe sat back and let out a happy sigh. "This was delicious. Next time we hit the Italian?"

"Sounds good to me." Esme smiled at her friend. Phoebe was a short, compact little package of sass, and had more self-confidence than Esme could ever dream of. "How do you do it, Pheebs? How do you stay so sure of yourself?"

Phoebe's eyes softened. "It's not always easy, you know. But if I don't love me, how can someone else? If I tear myself down, why shouldn't someone else? It sometimes takes some reminding, you know. But in the end… I treat myself the way I want others to treat me. With acceptance and love and a bit of a sense of humor."

"I wish I could manage that," Esme mourned, sitting back in her chair.

The waitress dropped off their checks and disappeared again, leaving a couple of mints behind. Esme grabbed one and popped it in her mouth.

"If I tell you my secret, you're sworn to silence," Phoebe answered, tucking her curtain of hair behind her ear.

"Duh," Esme replied.

"I write sticky notes to myself and put them on my bathroom mirror," she confessed. "And when I get up in the morning, I make myself say them out loud."

Esme considered that for a long moment. It didn't sound like the Phoebe she knew, but how could she ignore the proof that was right before her? Phoebe exuded confidence—not in a brash, arrogant way, but in an "I'm comfortable in my own skin" sort of way.

They paid their bills and parted ways after a quick hug on the sidewalk. Tomorrow she'd be back at Chatsworth Manor again, faced with Stephen. It was up to her to set the tone with him. She'd been the one to run away today. Before she went to sleep tonight, she had to decide exactly what she wanted from him and how she wanted to handle their relationship at the house.

By ten she was back in her own flat, listening to the silence that came from living alone. She hadn't wanted a roommate after the divorce, but now she wondered if she shouldn't ask the landlady if she could get a cat or something.

She flicked on the light to the bathroom and stared in the mirror. Big green eyes stared back at her, somber and perhaps a bit timid. She squared her shoulders and lifted her chin—better. She had no problem adopting this posture and attitude at work, but when it came to her own personal self-esteem… Esme frowned and put her hands on the edge of the vanity. Who was she kidding? Her self-esteem had been in the toilet for years.

There was a pad of sticky notes somewhere in a kitchen drawer. She marched to the kitchen and scrounged until she found them, slightly dusty, and a Sharpie marker. Then she stomped back to the bathroom, determination settling through her bones. She uncapped the marker and wrote on the first sticky "I am strong," then ripped it off the pad and stuck it to the mirror.

"I am strong," she said out loud. Huh.

On the next she wrote, "I am capable." Rip and stick.

More stickies followed.

"I am smart."

"I have a good heart."

"I am the perfect size for me." That one was a hard one, but she wrote it and stuck it on the mirror anyway. On and on she went, scribbling and sticking until the multicolored notes covered the mirror except for an oval where her face remained.

She wrote one more. "I have great hair," she said, and found an empty spot to stick it.

Then she stepped back. She'd gone a little overboard, but she did feel…stronger. With more resolve. Was this…confidence?

She gave her reflection a nod, and then flipped off the light switch. Tomorrow was an early day.

CHAPTER EIGHT

STEPHEN HAD BARELY slept, waking before six and staring at the ceiling. It was a strange feeling, being all alone in the house. Esme would be here later, but there were no maids, no kitchen staff…and the house was so very large. Empty. This week he'd spent more time alone with his thoughts than he had in…maybe ever.

He got up, pulled on a pair of sleep pants and a T-shirt, and headed down two flights to the kitchen. By six thirty he had a steaming cup of Colombian in his hands, the aroma warm and soothing.

Esme had left yesterday afternoon without a word, and he'd been on his own for dinner. It hadn't been a totally satisfactory meal. He'd slapped together a grilled cheese sandwich and made a salad from the vegetables in the fridge, but it wasn't the same as Esme's cooking. It filled the hole, though, so that was something.

She would be here in a few hours, and he had to decide what he was going to say to her.

He shouldn't have kissed her. She'd responded and then it had spooked her, hadn't it? Hell, it had spooked him, but he wasn't the one who'd run away.

He owed her an apology. Somehow they had to put their friendship back on solid ground again. He'd meant what he said about not having an overabundance of friends. Maybe he and Esme hadn't seen each other in years, but they'd picked up as if it hadn't been any time at all. She got him better than anyone he knew. He'd be a fool to jeopardize that, wouldn't he?

He brewed a second cup of coffee and went to shower, then attempted to make his bed as tidy and perfect as the maids did. He pulled the covers up as neatly as possible, fluffed the pillows, and went back to the kitchen to eat something for breakfast.

When Esme finally arrived at eight fifteen, he was already in the library, laptop booted up, answering the emails that had been streaming in.

She found him there a few minutes later. "Good morning. Sorry I'm a little late. Did you want some breakfast?"

He looked up and made himself smile, trying to make it relaxed and warm. "I managed breakfast already, thank you."

Her face flattened. "Oh! Well, good." A smile flitted on her lips, but it seemed unsure. She was feeling just as off-kilter as he was.

"Esme, why don't you grab a coffee and come back up? We should talk."

"Well, I…" She looked even more uncertain. "I do have work to get to…"

"It won't take long." He met her gaze evenly. "We need to clear the air, don't you think?"

She nodded, and something flickered in her eyes that he couldn't quite decipher. Still, Stephen figured being direct was the best approach. He really didn't know how to be anything else, he realized. And that probably made him…intimidating.

She slipped out of the library and he sat back in his chair, tapping his finger on his lower lip. Why was he so blunt? Why wasn't he more easygoing, like William, or charming like his cousin, Christophe? He supposed it came with the weight of responsibility, but he rather suspected it might be something more.

He looked over at the photo of his parents on the corner of the desk. His dad, tall, strong, with William's steady temperament and enough charm to work a room and leave everyone feeling as if they were basking in his glow. His mother, regal, smart, and elegant, but with a hint of devilment around her lips and her unique rusty laugh. It was impossible to follow in either of their footsteps. Stephen had tried very hard to not be like either of his parents. To be someone different and yet still live up to all the expectations that came with being the eldest and heir.

"You know the only person putting those expectations on you is you," came a voice from in front of him.

Esme, cradling a steaming cup of coffee. She'd caught him staring at the photo, but how on earth had she been able to read his mind?

"I don't know what you mean," he said, picking up his own cup and taking a sip.

"You're a horrible liar. You try to be all nonchalant, but it backfires. It always did." She pulled up a chair and sat down. "So what's bothering you?"

He frowned. "Nothing." Except that if he wasn't like his father, or like his mother, and he'd been trying to be so different, who really was he? Did he even know?

"You're thinking way too hard for someone who says nothing," she said. "But that's your business." She took a breath. "I'm sorry I ran from you yesterday. It wasn't the right way to handle what happened."

Apparently he wasn't the only one who could be forthright. Granted, her cheeks were a little pink and he got the feeling she wasn't exactly comfortable with broaching the topic, but she was doing it anyway.

"I was out of line," he admitted. "I got caught up in the moment, that's all."

"We're not ten anymore," she said, giving a nod. "We had no business being in that fort in the first place." Then her cheeks flushed deeper.

"Well, at least I didn't. Of course you can if you want. It's your fort."

His lips twitched. He was thirty-five and they were talking about a childhood fort. "We took a little time to rediscover our youth," he said, his voice a little warmer. "There's nothing terrible about that."

"Except you never kissed me in our youth."

His gaze snapped to hers. "You never kissed me, either."

Her lips dropped open a little at his quick reply. He hadn't been alone yesterday, and she'd definitely been a willing participant. The blame was mostly his, but not all of it.

"And now we're back where we started," she whispered.

He let out a sigh. "Esme... I'm sorry. It was wrong of me to kiss you. To get carried away. I'm only here for a short time and I'm honestly not looking for a relationship." He ignored the little voice in his head that reminded him how much he'd enjoyed their time at the pub and eating dinner here together two nights ago.

"I'm not either," she said. "Been there, done that. Have the divorce decree to prove it."

"That doesn't mean you shouldn't try again," Stephen reasoned, though he certainly didn't mean with him. Still, the thought of Esme alone for the rest of her life simply didn't fit. She had so much to offer the right man. Intelligence, beauty, a sharp sense of humor…

"Hello, Mr. Pot, meet Mr. Kettle." Esme lifted an eyebrow, then took a drink of her coffee.

Okay, so she had him there. "At least you actually made it through a ceremony," he groused, shaking his head.

She snorted.

Then her lush lips sobered. "Stephen, this… whatever happened yesterday, it's not real. I'm glad to see you again. I want to be your friend. But anything else is…"

"Is what?" He didn't necessarily disagree, but he wanted to hear her take on it.

"We're too different. And it's just… I don't know. Nostalgia, I guess."

"Different because I'm an earl and you're not."

"Different because one of your suits costs more than my wardrobe. One bottle of wine for you is my grocery budget for the month. You make business deals worth millions, and I am one step up from cleaning hotel rooms for a living." She lifted her chin. "Not that there is a thing wrong with good, honest work, and I like my job a lot. I always liked the feeling of a pristine room, ready to welcome someone inside and make their stay special."

"You're a nurturer, like your mother." He shrugged one shoulder. "I am not."

"That's what I'm saying. We're just…different."

It should have been the end of it. They were both in agreement that there could be nothing between them, so why did he feel the urge to ask about their attraction? Because their mouths were saying one thing and their eyes another. The eye contact put them right back on that blanket yesterday afternoon, in that charged moment when they'd hovered only inches apart, waiting for someone to make the first move.

She looked away first, and that was when he knew.

She was lying.

He wasn't sure what to say—whether to call her on it or let sleeping dogs lie. The first would be like lighting a match to paper, sparking their chemistry again. The second was the more prudent course. Keep everything platonic and professional and get through the next week.

He met her gaze. "I've been called back to Paris for a few days."

"Oh. I see."

She didn't, and probably thought he was running away from her, when nothing could be further from the truth. "There's a social thing, and someone in the family needs to attend. Gabi's come down with some sort of bug and Bella is already at another event that evening. And Annie... well, Annie hasn't really started representing the family at functions yet."

"So it's up to you."

"It's literally an overnight in Paris, maybe two, then back here for the gooseberry festival." He smiled a little. "My social engagements cover a broad range of activities."

"I see. So you're not just…avoiding me?"

He leaned forward. "No." Stephen normally kept his feelings under lock and key, but he found himself admitting, "I would rather spend the evening at the pub with you, if I'm honest."

Her green eyes held his, even as her teeth worried her lower lip. "What's the point, if this isn't going anywhere?"

He closed his eyes for a brief moment and pinched the bridge of his nose. "I know. Still doesn't stop me wanting to spend time with you." He opened his eyes again and looked over at her. "Es, something's changed in me since I came home. It's been difficult, but it's also been good. I think I need to see it through, whatever it is. And what I know for sure is that you're helping me somehow."

She made a funny, dismissive sound and started to roll her eyes, but he stopped her. "No, I mean it. I've told you more in the last few days than I've told anyone about the pressures I'm under. You can't know how important that's been." He folded his hands together on top of the desk to keep from reaching out to her. "Come with me to Paris. I need a plus-one anyway. Let me do something for you as a thank-you for all you've done for me."

Her face blanked with alarm. "Paris? With you? You're mad. Besides, all I've done is my job."

"We both know that's not strictly true." Her blush deepened, and he got up from his desk and went around to the front, resting his hips against it as he looked down at her. "Esme, I hate going to these things alone. And lately I've been paired up with my mother. Which is mostly fine but after a while…having your mother as your date for the evening is a bit…" He hesitated, unsure of what word he wanted.

"Sad?" He stared at her, and she laughed a little. "Sorry."

"No, you're right. Listen, it's only a few hours. I'll shake some hands and make small talk. There'll be some food and definitely champagne. The good stuff."

Esme stood and faced him. "You realize this is exactly the kind of thing that Evan would have asked of me. Dress appropriately, smile, shake hands, drink champagne."

Stephen pushed away from the desk. "Forget it, then."

"You don't have to pout about it."

He wanted to say, "I'm not," but he knew his voice had sounded decidedly petulant. "I wouldn't ask you to be someone you're not. I thought you might enjoy the getaway, and I could have company for the event that I actually enjoy. But not if you compare me to him."

"That's not what I meant—"

"Isn't it? I can't be less of who I am any more than you can, Esme. And if you think I would ask you to something and treat you as some sort of accessory, then you don't know me at all."

He went back around his desk and sat down again, his heart pounding against his ribs.

"I didn't say I wouldn't go," she whispered.

His gaze snapped back up to hers. She looked contrite, and a little scared, and perhaps even slightly defiant.

"I just said that this was something Evan would have asked me to do. No, not asked. Expected. And he would have made sure I understood I was not to embarrass him."

"The more I hear about your ex, the more I'd like to meet him," Stephen said darkly.

She went to him then, and rested against the desk beside his chair. "I know how to behave in social situations. I wouldn't embarrass you, and I know that. Any hesitation is because, well, I don't enjoy being under the microscope. It just invites comments that echo all my insecurities."

He couldn't assure her otherwise. He'd been in the spotlight his whole life and knew what it was like. "I understand," he replied.

She reached out and touched his arm. "Will there be press there?"

"Almost assuredly."

"And so my presence with you would open us up to speculation."

It wasn't that he didn't understand what she was getting at. It was more that he couldn't possibly live his entire life hiding from the paparazzi. She, however, could. "Look, Esme, it's fine if you don't want to go. I just thought it would be nice. I've done a million of these things before and survived."

He turned his attention back to his open laptop and touched his mouse to bring it back to life.

He was shutting her out.

Not that she blamed him. He'd invited her to Paris and she'd immediately put up roadblocks. Legitimate ones, she supposed, but she didn't doubt his motives. She believed him when he expressed his appreciation for listening to him, and despite her misgivings, she was flattered that he would even consider taking her to some function as his plus-one.

"Where would I stay?" she asked softly.

His fingers paused over his keyboard. "Wherever you like. At a hotel, or there's a spare room at my flat. Wherever you'd be most comfortable."

A spare room. Not his room, then. She was both relieved and disappointed. Because she could repeat the word *friend* as often as possible in her mind, but it didn't wash away the beating of her heart when he looked into her eyes, or erase the taste of his lips against hers just yesterday.

Ugh, she was in so much trouble. She didn't do casual, he didn't do love, she'd never fit in his world, and yet her need for him was under her skin, like an itch she couldn't scratch. She wanted to go. Perhaps…just this once?

"I would need time to go shopping for a dress," she said. She couldn't believe she was actually considering this. Wasn't it exactly what she'd said she didn't want? And yet, the way he'd kissed her yesterday…what if this time it was different? What if she was letting something from her past ruin something that could be really great? It would be foolish to give what was done that sort of power, wouldn't it?

He turned and looked up at her. "You're certain?"

She nodded. "I can't hide away in this village forever, can I? And how often does one get invited to Paris?" She gave her head a shake. "I mean someone like me."

"Don't worry about a dress. What's the sense of working in fashion if I can't whip up a stylist at a moment's notice?"

A stylist? For her? She'd shopped at some nice stores and been to some swanky dos, but she'd never had a stylist. Oh, she might be getting in over her head…

Just like that, her bubble burst. "I never thought. I'm not sure I can leave Mum."

"It's twenty-four, maybe forty-eight hours. I'm sure she'll be fine. Is there someone who can look in on her?"

"Her friend, Judy, I suppose."

"And it's Paris. If anything happens, I can have you back here in a couple of hours."

"What about…" Her face heated and she moved a finger between the two of them. "After yesterday…"

He got up from his desk slowly, and her breath caught as he stood mere inches away. She had to look up to see his face, and the moment she did, she had the urge to simply melt into his arms.

This would not do.

"Must we label it?" he asked, his low voice barely above a whisper. "Let's just be honest. I'm attracted to you, and if yesterday is any indication, you're attracted to me. Let's just see what happens. And if it gets to be too much, no hard feelings."

No hard feelings.

Her breath stuttered. He lifted his hand and slid it into her hair at the nape of her neck, then dropped his head and touched his lips to hers. Soft, gentle, seductive.

She was on fire.

Her reaction to him was like nothing she'd ever experienced. Never this burning need, the urge to dispense with clothes and feel his skin on hers, to be in his arms, become his lover. The urgency stole her breath, but she stood before him, barely moving, while the maelstrom of desire stormed within her.

She could stay in a hotel. Or in a room in his flat. What if she wanted to stay in his bed?

She was getting way ahead of herself. But she couldn't stop herself from responding to his kiss.

He stepped back, pressed his forehead to hers in a gesture that was surprisingly tender. "The event is tomorrow night. Can you be ready to leave in the morning?"

She nodded briefly, thinking she'd abandoned all sense and caution.

And then she slid out of his embrace and left the study, knowing she suddenly had a lot to do before she took the biggest risk of her life.

CHAPTER NINE

TELLING HER MUM she was off to Paris had been tricky. No matter how much Esme emphasized that she was going as a friend, Mary had that knowing look in her eye and a set to her lips that spoke of disapproval. It was almost as if she'd seen into Esme's brain and had known about the kisses she and Stephen had shared.

But they were both stubborn women, and Esme didn't change her mind, and Mary of course agreed that she could manage just fine for a few days without Esme's "hovering." Esme went home, packed a small bag for two nights, and met Stephen the next morning at the estate.

A driver took them to Gatwick, where a chartered plane zipped them off to Paris. Esme tried not to gawk. She'd been to some pretty upscale events as Evan's wife, but nothing like a hired jet to another country. Clearing customs was a whiz and before she knew it, she and Stephen were at his flat in the heart of the City of Light.

He smiled at her, opened the door, and swept his hand to the side, ushering her in.

Esme stood in the foyer, her eyes wide as she took in the sumptuous space. Stephen's apartment was spacious and modern, despite the building being old and venerable. She put down her bag and wandered in, admiring the crisp and clean décor. Off-white walls and large windows added to the open feel, and the kitchen, to her left, had state-of-the-art stainless-steel appliances and a wide counter for prepping meals. The kitchen led into a lovely dining room with a table that seated eight surrounded by plush chairs.

There was a big-screen television and a rich cream sofa for relaxing in the living room, with other wing chairs in vibrant fabrics adding a splash of color. There were also three bedrooms, each with their own bathroom. Stephen had made one of the bedrooms into an office, leaving a spare room and the main bedroom—his.

He had picked up her bag, and now placed it in the spare room. He truly wasn't making any assumptions, and she appreciated it. Now that she was here, nerves and doubts crowded into her heart and mind. Could she really do this? Could she be in this kind of world again, and still be... Esme?

Then she looked at Stephen and felt such a rush of emotion she knew she wanted to try.

Esme turned around, admiring it all. It was a

different sort of opulence from the manor house, and unfamiliar. Still, it suited him somehow. It was restful, rather than sparse. She liked it a lot. She liked him a lot.

"Welcome to Paris," he said, and he pulled her close, kissing her long and slow.

"Mmm." Her heart hammered with pleasure at the gentle but seductive welcome. "Let me go out and come back in again. That was nice."

He chuckled against her lips. "I'm hoping if I kiss you long enough, you won't be nervous about this evening."

"I'm going to be nervous anyway, but kissing you isn't a hardship."

He stepped back, took her hands in his, and held her gaze. "You don't have to come. If it's too much, I understand."

She squeezed his fingers. "I think I have to try. But—" She let go of his hands and sighed. "Can we talk first, before this stylist has a go at me? Because I think... I want you to understand where I'm coming from a little more." She swallowed tightly, afraid of her next words but knowing they were true. "I want to trust you with this."

He nodded. "Of course we can talk."

She didn't want to do this in her bedroom, so she skirted past him to the living room, where she could look out the wide windows at the city below. The view was stunning, and she took a deep breath, letting the view anchor her as she considered what she was going to share with him.

"It can't be that bad," he said, coming up behind her.

She turned to face him. The slight frown on his face was momentarily intimidating, but then she realized he wasn't frowning *at* her but rather *for* her and whatever unpleasant information she was about to share.

"It's not that bad," she said, trying to lighten things a little. "You already know a lot about my marriage to Evan…most of the important bits, anyway. This is more about what it did to me personally…on a self-esteem level, because going to this event with you tonight is more than not wanting to feel like arm candy. You see, when Evan had functions and dinners and whatnot, he always had opinions on what I wore, how I did my hair…if something was flattering, if I'd put on a few pounds, even what I was eating. I could order dessert or have it before me, but I could only have a few bites. He didn't like certain styles. I was never allowed to wear jeans. Those kinds of comments don't just go away when you sign your name on the divorce decree. I try to ignore them most of the time. But a night like tonight, where I'm going to be in a fancy dress and among beautiful people…it brings a lot of it back."

Instead of the frown disappearing, it deepened,

and a muscle ticked in his jaw. "So you're doing this to prove something to yourself?"

"In a way, I suppose I am."

He gave a brisk nod. "Good."

"Good?" She was surprised at his answer.

"Yes, absolutely. You've told me that I need to step out of my father's shadow, and I don't need to carry the weight of his actions. I realized that no one can do that but me, and no one can do this for you but you." His dark eyes were bright with resolve. "And if going to this thing tonight is helping you do that, I'm one hundred percent onboard."

Tears sprang into her eyes. Nothing had prepared her for his unqualified support. He wasn't trying to fix anything. He wasn't trying to tell her how wrong Evan had been. Instead, he'd validated every single one of her feelings and then basically said he'd be beside her while she dealt with them.

No one—not even her mother—had offered this kind of support. It was what the old Stephen would have done when they were kids. It was why she'd liked him. He'd always—with the exception of the day he said goodbye to her—treated her as an equal.

If he kept this up, she was going to fall for him—hard.

"Don't cry," he said, his voice gentle. "He's not worth crying over."

"That's not why." She sniffled. "You just…reminded me of the Stephen I used to know. I like that person a lot."

"He happens to like you a lot, too. But if I don't get you over to Aurora, you're going to be late for your appointment."

"I am?"

He nodded. "You are. And for the rest of today, you're not to worry about a thing."

From the outside, it looked like a simple cocktail party, with the usual wine, champagne and tiny but delectable finger foods. But Stephen knew that inside were some of the biggest players in European exports. The host was a well-known billionaire, and one did not turn down an invitation—not even if one was a Pemberton. Stephen slid his right hand into his pocket as he stood outside the small ballroom, waiting for Esme. She'd texted and said they were running a little behind, but that she would meet him here. It was now a half hour past the time on the invitation, making her fashionably late.

Normally this wouldn't faze him in the least. But it was Esme. And he was worried she'd got cold feet.

He cradled a glass of Scotch in his left hand, but he'd taken a single obligatory sip and that was it. He was too nervous and distracted. Just as he was ready to take out his mobile and send her a text, the elevator doors opened, and she stepped out.

His heart stopped for a second, then started beating again in a fast tattoo.

The dark green silk clung to her curves, dropping in a simple column over her hips to the floor. The V neckline and wide straps on her shoulders revealed the creamy, soft skin of her neck and arms, and the stylist had done the world a favor and left Esme's hair down, letting it fall in glorious copper waves and ripples that framed her face and whispered along her back.

This was the same Esme who donned plain black trousers and a button-down black shirt for work. Who pulled her hair back in a no-nonsense braid or bun as she managed the manor staff. She was utterly transformed, and yet exactly the same. She was, and always had been, magnificent.

"Wow. You… Esme. You take my breath away."

She smiled, her eyes lighting up. "You like it? Patrice said green is my color."

He figured any color would be her color, but he couldn't deny the jewel tone suited her. "You're stunning." He swallowed against a surprising lump in his throat and tried a smile. "And in need of champagne, I think."

She looped her arm through his and they entered the ballroom. No expense had been spared; exotic flowers bloomed from every corner and at the center of each table. Candles sent flickering light through the opulent space. There was enough champagne flowing to fill a swimming pool, and glittering jewels sparkling at every throat. Every throat except Esme's, he realized. The stylist had picked the perfect Aurora couture gown and shoes, had ensured Esme's hair and makeup were flawless, but she was missing Aurora gems. He imagined her wearing one of Sophie's creations, something as unique and special as she was, perhaps in diamonds and emeralds. But it would have been foolish to make such a gesture for a single cocktail party, wouldn't it? When they were just friends?

Except they weren't just friends. The way they'd kissed earlier today had made that abundantly clear. Maybe he wasn't in the market for a relationship, but he suspected he was caught in the middle of one anyway. As Esme smiled and sipped her champagne from a gold-rimmed flute, the thought simultaneously terrified and thrilled him.

"Are you all right?" she asked, lowering her glass. "What's wrong?"

"Nothing," he replied, schooling his features. It wouldn't do for him to walk around with his emotions written all over his face. "Come, I'll introduce you to a few people."

They made their rounds and he shook the hands of all the people he knew he should. Champagne was drunk and refilled, but Esme turned down the offer of any food, and he thought he detected some strain around the edges of her smile. When she'd offered the seventh "Nice to meet you"—or was it eighth?—he swept her away from the crowd and onto the dance floor.

She felt so right in his arms, and as he made a small turn in time to the music, he felt her relax a little. "Sorry," he whispered near her ear. "I know it's a lot."

"It's fine. A little too familiar, perhaps." She leaned back a little and met his gaze. "I guess I… oh, never mind."

"You guess what? You can tell me."

She sighed, then looked up at him again. "I guess I just prefer a more genuine connection. I'm not one for show."

"And thank God for that," he said, as a new thought struck him. He kept his feet moving, guiding her in smooth, small steps, but he made sure to hold her gaze. "You wouldn't be you if you enjoyed the superficial. This is business tonight, but that's all. It's not…real. You understand that. Not everyone does. Some people think this is… I don't know. The goal."

"Like Bridget?"

He nodded, his throat tight. "I just didn't see it at first. This isn't me, Es. Oh, it's part of what I do. It goes with the position. But it's not me, in here." He let go of her hand and touched his heart, then took her fingers in his again. "You do know that, don't you?"

She bit down on her lip a little, then released

it before she spoke again. "I do. You're so much more than this."

"And so are you," he murmured, his gaze dropping to her lips. He wouldn't kiss her here. He understood without her having to say so that she'd prefer to keep private things private. But he wanted to, and as he lifted his gaze, he saw by the flush in her cheeks that she understood.

"Thirty minutes," he said, his voice husky. "Give me thirty minutes to finish the duty rounds and we can be out of here."

She laughed softly. "I spent three hours getting ready for one hour and a few glasses of champagne?"

"I didn't say the night was over."

Her lips fell open as the song ended and he released her. From the moment she'd said yes to this trip, something had changed between them. Once they left the hotel, it would just be the two of them for the rest of the night. He couldn't think past that. For once, he was going to do as she suggested. He was going to lay down all his burdens. And in the morning, he'd decide which ones he would pick up again.

Esme had been nervous about the cocktail party, but that was nothing compared to how she felt now, after Stephen's last words.

The night wasn't over.

They sped through the Paris evening, the soft

part of the day where the world seemed washed in pinks and violets. Stephen said nothing, but his fingers were twined with hers on the leather seat of the car's interior. Esme was so aware of him, of herself, that her breasts tingled against the silk of her dress and her stomach fluttered with nerves—anticipation, surely, as well as hesitation, because without saying so, she knew tonight her relationship with Stephen was going to change.

She wanted him. Wanted him so much she ached with it.

When they finally arrived at his building, he held out his hand and helped her out of the car, then let his palm rest on the hollow of her back, a warm, electric touch that skittered over her nerve endings and gave her goose bumps as the silk dress slid over her skin. The underwear Patrice had given her to wear—Aurora lingerie, naturally—was so tiny it was almost as if she weren't wearing any at all. The seductive slide of the fabric over her hypersensitive skin only added to her arousal—and Stephen hadn't even touched her yet. Not really.

But he was going to. She knew it as surely as she knew she was ready for him.

The flat was dark, and Stephen reached for a light switch, but she stayed his hand with her own. Twilight shimmered through the windows, lighting the flat intimately. Esme put down her clutch on a small table and turned to face him, shocked and thrilled by the naked yearning on his face.

She'd been dying to touch him for hours. The tension crackled, snapping between them like an arc of electricity. Attraction. Need. Desire. The fire in his eyes burned as brightly as hers, and in one breathtaking moment he gathered her in his arms and did what she'd been dying for all evening: kissed her silly.

The air between them had been thick like thunderclouds and opened up in a downpour of passion. After the first initial clash of lips and tongues he pulled away, but her hands yanked him back in. She followed his mouth with her own, nipping at his lower lip, and her hands went to his shirt, fumbling with the buttons.

They might be on the verge of making a huge mistake, but she was past caring. Not when her need for him was this sharp. And God, what a revelation. She felt so…alive. He made her feel so sexy and desirable, something that had been missing from her life for far too long.

His shirt gaped open and she ran her hands over his hard chest. He tangled his fingers in her hair and slid his hot mouth down the curve of her neck, making her gasp with pleasure. In one quick motion, he slid his hands down to cup her bottom, then lifted her and deposited her on the edge of the dining table.

"Esme," he growled, sliding his hands into her

hair, holding her head steady as he kissed her again.

The slim column of her dress was restrictive, so she reached back to try to undo the zipper. Once Stephen realized what she was doing, he covered her fingers with his and slid the zipper to her waist. She shimmied out of the bodice of the gown, felt the cool air on her breasts as he flicked open the clasp on the tiny bra.

"I love your freckles," he whispered, sliding his mouth down her neck again, bending to her and tasting her sensitive skin. She could hardly breathe and leaned back, bracing herself on her hands as she opened for his touch.

But it wasn't enough. Only moments later he pulled her to her feet, and the emerald silk fell to the floor in a luxurious heap, leaving her standing in nothing but a barely-there thong and the stilettos Patrice had slipped onto her feet.

Stephen stared, and then he swore. The words were possibly the most erotic thing she'd heard in her life. She, Esme Flanagan, had reduced the great Stephen Pemberton to near speechlessness. The hunger in his eyes was so thrilling she thought she might melt from the heat of it.

They had to slow down. Make it good and not just fast. Especially if this was their one and only night. Nothing had changed. She just didn't care about the issues as much as she wanted him.

"Es," he whispered, more than a little awe in his voice. "Are you sure?"

She met his gaze with her own as she spoke her truth. "I've never been more sure of anything in my life."

"Es," he said again, the import of what she'd just admitted settling over them both.

"Don't think," she whispered, stepping toward him. "Don't talk if that's going to ruin what this is. Just let it be, if it's what you want." She swallowed. "If I'm what you want."

"I'm not the kind to make rash decisions. Every move I make is precisely thought out with cool calculation. But there's nothing cool between you and me, Es. It's a five-alarm fire burning out of control. But I want it. I want you."

"Just for tonight," she murmured, stepping closer to him. "I want to stop thinking, stop analyzing. I want to feel instead, and I want to feel you. I've waited so long, Stephen."

She reached for him, running her fingertips along his chest while his breath stalled. Her nails marked his skin lightly, and she was close enough now that her breasts rubbed against him, the feel of skin on skin so incredibly perfect. He caught her hand with his and kissed her fingers, then met her gaze. "Esme, I don't have protection. I can't… we can't…"

Esme traced her other hand over his face. "I'm on birth control."

Stephen swept her up into his arms and into his bedroom, where he laid her down on the soft duvet. She looked up, watched as he took off his tuxedo trousers and then his boxer briefs.

And when he joined her on the bed, she stopped thinking altogether, and gave herself over to the sensations of being his lover.

CHAPTER TEN

ESME ROLLED OVER in the bed and found the other side empty, but there was a dent in the pillow next to her. She'd slept here, in Stephen's bed. They'd made love again in the middle of the night, slower that time, and Esme had eventually fallen into a deep, satisfied sleep.

Water ran in the bathroom… Stephen's shower. For a moment she considered slipping beneath the hot spray with him, but in the light of day common sense…caution…reared its ugly head.

What on earth had they been thinking last night?

She needed to get up. Go back to her room, have a shower, and change her clothes. If she hurried, she could be dressed and ready for the day before he came out of his bathroom.

Except she didn't exactly want to run, even though she was afraid of what this meant for their…relationship. She didn't know how to feel. It had been the most amazing night of her life— and she included her wedding day in that assessment—but the fairy tale was over. Besides, if Stephen had wanted her to share his shower, he would have awakened her. He was probably just as anxious for her to be on her way as she was. They'd got caught up in the moment, that was all. Wasn't it?

Oh, God. This was going to be so awkward.

She scrambled out of bed, belatedly realizing she was stark naked. She moved quickly, trying to find her underwear. Nothing. Her dress and bra were probably still by the dining table. And her panties...

Stephen appeared at the door of the bathroom, where he stood wearing nothing but a thick, white towel. Her mouth literally watered at the sight of him, but she pushed the reaction aside.

A smile crawled up his cheek. "Looking for this?" he offered. The tiny string of the thong was looped over his finger.

She snatched up the sheet from the bed and held it over herself. Stephen burst out laughing, the sound so foreign and wonderful she couldn't stop the shy smile that curved her lips.

"You don't need to be embarrassed," he said gently, coming into the bedroom.

She avoided his gaze, wondering how to gracefully exit to her own room and the clothing that awaited there. "This is very new territory for me, that's all."

"I'm glad. For me, too."

She wondered if it was, really. He was a rich, handsome man. But then, she rather thought he meant it. The Stephen she knew wasn't the kind to indulge in random hookups. Instead he'd practically come right out and admitted he was lonely.

She couldn't seem to make herself go to the door, but she couldn't stand around in a sheet all day, either. "We, uh, might have got carried away last night."

He came closer. "Do you have regrets?"

She could say yes and this would all end now. One glorious night to tuck away in the memory banks. But the truth was, she didn't regret it. How could she when it had been perfect? The problem was it was so perfect it scared the daylights out of her. She had zero idea where to go from here.

"No," she whispered. "Do you?"

He shook his head. "I don't. I probably should. You and I…we go back too far for this to be a hookup. And if it's not a hookup…"

More panic cramped her lungs and made her head light. "What are you suggesting…that we start dating or something?"

She realized belatedly that she'd made it sound like a preposterous idea, which perhaps it was, but she didn't mean to sound so harsh. "Stephen, what I mean is—"

He went to a wardrobe, opened the door, and pulled out a shirt. "You know, this is very strange for me. All of my life, people have gotten close to me for what I could do for them. Sometimes it was just to be seen with me. Not just for the title—titles aren't as big a deal now as they were a century ago—but because of Aurora and all the money. But you don't want anything from me. Not even what I want to give you. I don't know if I should be insulted or relieved."

"Not insulted. Please, Stephen, don't think that." Ugh, they were going to have to have a whole discussion about it, weren't they? How could they not, after what had transpired last night? She'd been a willing participant...more than willing. There'd been a sense that they'd been heading in that direction all along. But now they had to deal with it. Just not right this minute.

"We need to talk," she admitted, shoving her hair back from her face. "But please...let me go for now. I need a shower, and clean clothes, and not to do this while dressed in...in a sheet."

He dropped the towel and gave her one delicious look at his backside before pulling on a pair of boxers.

The fact that his dark eyes now held what she interpreted as hurt made her feel guilty. But that was ridiculous, wasn't it? She couldn't possibly have the power to hurt him. She tried to relax a little. "I'll be back, okay? I just really need to clean up and get my bearings again. Last night was..." She trailed off, unsure of how to finish her sentence. Incredible? Absolutely. Unbelievable? In more ways than one. But it was really just a lot. She was feeling quite overwhelmed.

"Okay," he said, but she saw a muscle tick in his jaw. He wasn't as chill about this as the single word let on.

Esme slipped out of the room, leaving him behind, then shut the door as quietly as possible before hurrying across the hall. She swallowed against a lump in her throat. The morning after should have been lazy and sweet, with kisses before reluctantly tearing herself away from his arms. Instead, all she could see was expectation. Expectation to be someone she wasn't, to fit into his world if they took this beyond last night. And she had no idea how to explain it to him. She just knew she had to, because he deserved better.

Perhaps she needed to have a little faith in him. It was just hard when her faith and trust had been missing for years.

She took a quick shower, dressed and found Stephen in the kitchen, slicing fruit on a heavy cutting board.

"Hi," she said, feeling strangely shy. When she'd left he'd been in boxers, sitting on the bed where they'd been as intimate as two people could possibly be. It was quite different walking into a kitchen, seeing him dressed in trousers and a button-down, a knife in his hand and a pile of pineapple to one side.

"Feeling better?" he asked, looking over at her, a small smile on his face.

"Feeling more put together, anyway," she admitted, stepping closer.

"I made some breakfast for us. Sliced fruit, yogurt, and croissants. And coffee."

It looked delicious. "Sit down," he invited, leading her to the table. "Get some caffeine into you, and some food. You didn't even eat last night. You must be starving."

It was strange enough that the Earl of Chatsworth was waiting on one of the staff. But even if he hadn't had the title, being waited on was not something Esme had ever been familiar with. Evan had always just assumed that she would be the one to do those little things. He'd taken her nurturing side for granted, she realized, marveling as Stephen placed a steaming cup of coffee before her. As he went back to finish putting together their meal, she thought of how Evan had always been charming but somehow lacking in substance. Stephen, on the other hand, could be charming, could be a grouch, but he had layers that made him a complicated, caring man.

And she really had to stop comparing him to Evan. It was just that it was hard, because up until now, Evan had been her relationship yardstick.

"Breakfast is served," he said, bringing her a plate. There was a small bowl to one side with yogurt, artfully arranged fruit, and a flaky croissant. He returned with the butter dish and a jar of preserves.

"It looks wonderful," she said, still touched by his thoughtfulness. And he wasn't wrong. She was starving. Last night food had been the last thing on her mind.

She broke off a piece of pastry, buttered it, and added a dollop of jam. Flavor exploded on her tongue. A sip of the coffee proved to be hot and strong. Delicious. "You're spoiling me," she murmured. "And I don't deserve it."

"I disagree." He put down his cup and faced her. "Es, I understand morning-after jitters. Sex changes things. But I'm still me."

"Well, you're not exactly you. I mean, you've changed over the last week."

"How so?"

She popped another piece of croissant into her mouth. "Well, you've unclenched."

He laughed, the sound rich and happy. "I suppose. And I'll probably re-clench when I have to come back full-time and face all my responsibilities."

The reminder these few weeks were temporary deflated the mood, and Esme picked at her plate. "You don't have to, you know. Not if you've discovered some things that make you happier."

He reached across the table for her hand and twined his fingers with hers. "Like you, perhaps?"

Heat rushed up her face. "That's not what I meant—"

"But you are a big part of why I've relaxed. You know it's true."

"Yes, but I live and work back home. And you just pop in from time to time. Our lives are not even in the same country." Even as she said it, though, her hand stayed twined with his.

"Esme, last night…"

Here it comes. He was going to let her down easy, explain all the reasons why he cared for her, but they couldn't have a repeat of last night. She agreed with it all, so why did knowing what was coming cause a hollow pit in her stomach?

"Last night was…really good." He tightened his fingers, and when she looked into his eyes she was surprised to see a flicker of…could that be vulnerability? It seemed impossible. Stephen didn't do vulnerable. But there was an uncertainty there, an openness she hadn't expected. "I just mean… not just the sex, though that was pretty fantastic." His cheeks grew ruddy and she added embarrassment to her list of surprising emotions from Stephen. "But you… I don't trust many people in the world, but you've known me longer than almost anyone. That made it…special."

She gave a small laugh, and admitted, "I don't know what to say."

"I know. But you should know, Esme, that being with you…"

"For me, too," she whispered. "And it kind of scares me to death."

They'd both forgotten about the lovely meal he'd prepared as they stared at each other, linked by their joined hands. Uncertainty swam in Esme's belly. This couldn't go anywhere, couldn't end well, could it? So why hadn't she got up from the table and moved away? Why had she just admitted her feelings…or at least one of the many feelings rushing through her right now?

Because it was Stephen. And she trusted him, too. Regardless of money or status or expectation. He was just…different.

"You should know," she began softly, "that I haven't really dated much since my divorce. Leaving Evan was a big act of defiance for me, but that doesn't mean I don't have scars. I do. As hard as I try to overcome them, they never quite go away."

His dark gaze hardened. "He didn't treat you right." After a beat he asked, "Physically?"

"No," she answered, shaking her head. "No, he never hit me. But he put me down a lot. I never felt good enough. I was always too fat, too thin, my hair was wrong, my clothes were wrong…or we never had enough money, or I didn't make him what he wanted to eat…"

Stephen swore.

She smiled. "Precisely. But I never stood up for myself, either. If he said I was overweight, I tried a new diet. If he didn't like dinner, I'd make something else."

"He could have made his own dinner," Stephen interrupted.

"Absolutely. But when your self-esteem is in the toilet, your brain doesn't work that way. I was not as strong as I should have been. But to everyone, we looked like the perfect couple. When I walked away, people kept telling me I was crazy." She sighed and looked up at him. "Even my mother. The only people who know what it was really like are my best friend, Phoebe, and now you. And I've only told you because you say you trust me and last night things changed between us."

"You don't think I…" He let the word hang.

"Of course not. At least, I don't think you'd mean to," she said gently, rubbing her thumb over his hand. "But if we started seeing each other… The world you live in, it's so visible. It's filled with beautiful people, and I would feel the burden of that expectation to be perfect. Maybe you wouldn't impose it, but you know perfectly well that I'd be under a microscope. I'm going to use the biggest cliché in the world, but it's really true. It's not you. Any woman would be lucky to be with you. It's me. I don't think I'm up to this."

Silence fell between them. Then Stephen spoke into the awkward pause.

"I'm so sorry that happened to you, Esme. You deserved so much better."

It was the last thing she expected him to say. She'd expected him to say that it wouldn't be that way, all the empty reassurances and platitudes that changed nothing. Instead, he simply empathized with her, and the fact that he believed, cared, and acknowledged her issues meant so much.

She could fall for this Stephen very easily.

She pulled her hand away. "It is what it is, as Mum likes to say. I've worked really hard the last few years to overcome some of my issues. It wouldn't be smart to put myself in the kind of environment that would challenge all of that hard work."

"Of course not." He pulled his hand back, but his gaze never left hers. "And yet...there is something between us. Something more than childhood friends. Esme, I haven't had that kind of chemistry—"

She got up from the table abruptly. "Can we perhaps talk about this later? I'm still trying to sort it all out in my mind."

He nodded. "Don't go. Finish your breakfast." Then he crossed his heart. "I promise I won't bring up the fantastic sex we had last night."

She snorted out a laugh, she couldn't help it. He looked positively boyish. If only the paparazzi caught him like this, instead of always looking so severe...

But the thought sobered her quickly enough. She imagined dating him and being caught on camera. What would they say about her, where she came from, what she looked like? Just the thought of that kind of scrutiny made her chest cramp with anxiety. Oh, why couldn't he just be...normal?

She sat back down, stabbed a grape with her fork. "Only because I'm hungry."

Stephen smiled, but within seconds he was serious again. "Es, would it really be so bad, being with me? You know me, you know my family. I'd at least like to give us a chance."

She swallowed the grape, her emotions a turmoil inside her. She wanted to...oh, how she wanted to. Last night with Stephen had been amazing. She'd laughed more this past week, felt more alive...but a few weeks in the summer was not the same as a serious relationship. "I don't think I'm ready for a relationship," she admitted softly. "Not even with you, Stephen. I like you. I trust you more than I trust any man, because I've known you longer. But a relationship... I'm not up to that. I'm sorry."

He nodded, disappointment etched on his features. "Me, too. And that's it for me, too, you know. I gave up on relationships. My trust level was near zero. But you... We have history together." He swallowed, his throat bobbing. "Thank you. For being honest. Even if the answer isn't what I wanted."

But had she been honest? Only partially. The other part of her wanted to ignore the past, ignore her problems. She'd had a crush on him as a boy but now that he was a man? She could see herself falling in love so easily—and could see herself getting her heart broken just as easily.

"You're a good man, Stephen."

"I'm not so sure."

"You are. Maybe you just need to give people a break." She met his gaze. "Stop expecting them to let you down like Bridget did." She leaned forward, peered into his eyes a little closer. "Like your dad did."

Stephen pushed his plate aside. "Yeah. I'm having trouble with the memorial in my mind. If my mother could forgive him, why can't I?"

"Because our childhood heroes are on pedestals," she whispered. Little did he know that he was *her* childhood hero. And he was up on that pedestal, too. She refused to believe he would ever disappoint her, though. He had far too much integrity. "What your dad did hurt you, but you would never do what he did. That's why you can't understand it, and why it makes you angry."

He nodded. "And I can't change it. It certainly isn't Anemone's fault."

Stephen rose from the table and began collecting their dishes. "Now," he said, his voice a bit brighter, "let's leave all this heaviness behind. What would you like to do today?"

He was laying Paris at her feet. What would he say if she wanted to do the most stereotypical things possible? She'd been to the city a handful of times, but Evan had always insisted the touristy stuff was too "pedestrian."

"I'd like coffee at an outdoor café. I'd like to walk the Champs d'Elysées and see the Eiffel Tower."

He smiled at her. "Consider it done."

"You don't mind?"

He shrugged. "Why on earth would I mind?"

That was it. She really had to stop painting him with Evan's brush.

"You got breakfast. I'll tidy up and get ready, then. You're sure it's okay? You don't have to go into work today?"

"Work can wait," he answered, picking up his empty plate. "As someone told me recently, the world won't end if I don't handle everything myself."

She watched him put his plate in the sink and gave a little sigh. She'd told him she wasn't up for a relationship, but this certainly felt like the beginnings of one. Maybe they weren't spending the morning in bed, but they were going to roam through Paris together. It certainly felt…couple-y.

Tomorrow they'd be back in England. Would it be so bad to pretend for one more day?

CHAPTER ELEVEN

STEPHEN HAD NEVER really played tourist in Paris. He'd become acquainted with the city when he was a small child, and it had become a second home. But seeing it through Esme's eyes was something special.

She was something special. And it wasn't just the fireworks from last night, though they'd been spectacular. It was how he felt just being in the same space as her. Calmer. Happier. Definitely less stressed. The weight of the world wasn't quite so heavy when she smiled at him.

Now they'd stopped at a small café just as she'd wanted, sipping on small cups of espresso and nibbling on macarons and madeleines.

Esme let out a satisfied sigh and turned her face up to the early afternoon sunshine. "This has been the most perfect day."

"I'm glad." He popped the rest of a lemon and lavender macaron in his mouth, washing it down with a swallow of the strong coffee. "Though I can't believe you wanted to take the stairs at the tower."

She grinned at him, and it was like he was hit with a ray of sunshine. "You kept up. Well done."

And they'd walked along the Champs d'Elysées, just as she'd wanted. When he would have suggested a sensible lunch, she'd declared that it was dessert first day.

On the way back to the flat, he was going to take her shopping. She couldn't come to Paris and not shop a little.

Their coffees were refilled, and they were chatting about the memorial garden plans when his phone buzzed. A quick check showed it was from Maman. He scrolled through, his frown deepening. He was being summoned to a family dinner at Christophe and Sophie's. No excuses. Everyone was going to be there. Oh, and Esme was very welcome to join. It was a family dinner but casual.

Reading between the lines, there was something Maman wasn't saying. Tension settled across his brow. Could they not go a month without having some sort of family announcement?

"What is it? You look like you got bad news."

"Not bad news exactly. More of a summons." He shrugged. "Maman messaged to say the family is getting together at Christophe's tonight and attendance is mandatory."

Esme chuckled, and he sent her a dark look. "Okay," she relented, still chuckling. "I shouldn't laugh at you getting a summons from your mother."

He smiled reluctantly. "I might be the earl, but Maman is the head of the family. And it might seem like a summons, but the truth is, we'd all go to the ends of the earth for her."

"Like I would for my mum," she murmured.

"Exactly." Fondness for both their mothers flooded his heart. "I might not understand all her choices, but I love her."

"Of course you do. That's why it's so hard." She reached over and put her soft hand on top of his briefly, then slid it away. "Anyway, don't worry about me. I'll be fine this evening."

"The invitation is also extended to you."

"Oh." Her eyes widened. "Oh."

Going to a family dinner…would it seem as if they were a couple? Did he want them to be? Or would it be something more like catching up? Esme wasn't exactly a stranger, at least not to his siblings.

"I understand if you feel like it's walking into the lion's den. I can make your excuses."

She twisted a macaron, separating the top from the bottom. "I'm assuming they know I was your plus-one last night."

"Maman does. And the rest probably do by now as well. But guess what? We managed to avoid being in the papers or online, thanks to your fashionably late arrival." He smiled, hoping his words would relax her a little. Instead, her lips tightened, and she fiddled with her napkin. "Esme? What is it?"

"I don't know. It just feels like…well, sneaking around isn't any way to live. And it reminds me that last night was a onetime thing but going in separate cars and hiding away isn't really a strategy for managing the press."

She was right. And he truly understood her aversion to the public eye, especially after what she'd told him about her history. Which left them exactly where they were before last night's party, with one glaring exception: they'd made love. And it had rocked his world.

"Maybe," he said gently, reaching for her hand, "we can take this day by day. No commitments, no expectations."

She twined her fingers with his. "I'd like that," she whispered. "I'd like that very much."

Relief rushed through him. And while he wanted her to go with him tonight, he knew he couldn't push. His family was a lot. He and Es were at a tenuous place. "And if you don't want to go tonight, I understand. Truly."

To his surprise, Esme lifted her chin. "Well, if I'm to go, I can't wear this." She looked down at her plain trousers and blouse. "I'll have to change."

"Let's do one better. Let's go shopping. We have time. Time for…lots of things."

She didn't miss his meaning as her gaze clung

to his and her cheeks pinkened. If they were going to take things day by day, he'd have to make sure each day was something special.

Esme put the finishing touches to her hair and makeup and ran her hands over her new dress. The navy linen held its shape, narrowing in a V-necked bodice and then falling to the tops of her knees in flat but feminine ruffles that gave the conservative cut a hint of whimsy. Neutral heels cushioned her feet, and she'd kept her makeup light and fresh. She didn't want to be too obvious, but wanted to look nice. Like she fit in. Taking a final, deep breath, she stepped out of her room and went to find Stephen.

He was waiting in the living room, standing by the window and looking out over the city. At the sound of her heels, he turned. "Wow. You look gorgeous. I know better than to kiss you and ruin your lipstick, though."

"I'd rather have the kiss," she answered, her stomach trembling with nerves both about the dinner and about kissing him. "I can fix lipstick."

"And that is what I like about you," he replied, dropping a light kiss in her lips.

They hopped in a hired car and made the trip to Christophe and Sophie's home in the sixteenth arrondissement, which made Esme goggle when she first saw it. Real estate in this part of the city had to be astronomical, and they'd chosen a house with a garden. It was like a little bit of heaven right in the city, and Esme couldn't keep her head from moving to and fro, taking in the lush grass, shrubs, and flowers that offered a little haven of privacy around the venerable home.

"They picked here because of the children," Stephen explained as they made their way to the front door. "There's just the one, now, but they want a family."

"It's stunning."

The door was answered by Sophie herself, holding the baby in her arms, a tiny package dressed in a pink frilly dress. She was still awake and looking around at everyone with wide brown eyes.

Introductions were made and drinks offered in a gorgeous room that had French doors overlooking the back garden. Esme had just accepted a glass of wine when Charlotte and Jacob arrived. Charlotte was animated and chatty while Jacob held back and just set adoring eyes on his wife. Charlotte was a bit intimidating. Like Stephen, she seemed to be rather Type A. But when she looked at her husband, her face softened. Esme liked that about her.

Then came Bella and Burke. Bella was CEO of Aurora but brought a relaxed vibe with her, and Burke was utterly charming. He and Will had gone to school together and Burke was, in addition to being a top cardiac doctor, Viscount Downham. More wine was poured, Aurora showed up at the same time as Will and Gabi, and the noise level in the house rose.

"Your family is huge."

"Bigger now with all the partners. And children." Stephen smiled at her. "And there's still Annie and Phillipe. You'll meet them soon, I hope."

Bella approached with a bottle of wine. "You look like you need a top-up, Esme," she said, pouring a bit more into Esme's glass. "And I love your dress. It really suits you. That cut is fabulous, and the navy highlights your skin."

"This is my cue," Stephen said dryly. "I deal with dollars, not hemlines."

Bella waved him away, then turned to Esme. "I'm not going to mince words, Esme. We're all so pleased you're here."

Her mouth fell open. "You are?"

Bella laughed and nodded. "Are you kidding? Stephen has been a bear for the past few years. He was horrible to Gabi after she left him at the altar. Which is sort of understandable, really, but he's just been so...dour." She made a face. "He's always been the serious one, but after Bridget, he seemed to be more...brittle. But one look at him tonight...he's relaxed and smiling and not just going through the motions. If spending time with you is the cause, we're all indebted to you."

Esme took a sip of her wine, partly to cover her face which had to be blushing now. But she was also feeling rather defensive on Stephen's behalf. "Oh, well… I guess he's had a lot to deal with since your dad died. I'm sure he doesn't mean to be…"

"Crabby? Grouchy? Bossy?"

Esme wasn't sure how much she should say, but she remembered Evan always schooling her to be bland and polite. That just wasn't her. She spoke her mind. "It can't be easy becoming the head of the family overnight, with the estate and the company to worry about." She tempered her words with, "If he's more relaxed, then I'm so glad. He's a good man."

"Oh, you've got it bad," Bella said, a smile lighting her face.

"Not at all," Esme lied. "But we've been friends a long time. I care about him."

There was a pause as they both took a drink of their wine. Then Bella sighed and put a hand on Esme's arm. "Would it be okay if I offered some advice? It can be hard being a part of this family, in the spotlight and knowing that strangers are going to delight in pointing out your flaws. Or taking something utterly normal and making it sound like a detriment." She pointed to her shoulders. "I stopped hiding my scars. I stopped giving away the power to own my own story. But I had Burke by my side. If you and Stephen do try to make a go of it, please remember that he'll be beside you. Don't let them own your story, Esme.

Live it and let the others be damned." She gave a brisk nod.

"It's reassuring knowing you don't all hate me."

"How could we? We all knew you when we were little. You were always bright and fun. Stephen needs that in his life. And you're right, he's a good man. He'll be good to you, you know. He feels things very deeply, so if he says he loves you, you can believe it's true."

Esme's cheeks heated again. "Oh, there's nothing like that." Maybe there was for her, but she was certain Stephen wasn't in love with her. Care? For sure. And there was no denying their chemistry was off the charts. But love? Everything she knew about the Stephen of today was that he had closed himself off to that particular emotion.

"Hmm. Maybe. Now come on, Sophie was a smart new mum and had dinner catered. I think everything has arrived."

Esme followed Bella into the state-of-the-art kitchen and discovered Charlotte, Gabi, Sophie and Aurora all there, unpacking delicious-smelling containers. Sophie was dispatched to the dining room with plates and flatware, while Christophe fed the baby a bottle and the men took over uncorking and pouring wine. Before long they were all settled at the long table in the dining room, with scrumptious smells wafting up from the serving dishes.

Will stood up. "Attention, loud family!"

All the chatter ceased, and their eyes turned to Will.

"Sophie, do you have Annie on FaceTime?"

Sophie nodded and propped up her tablet. "Say hi, Annie!"

Annie and Phillipe waved from their home in Grasse.

Will cleared his throat. "Thank you to Sophie and Christophe for hosting tonight's dinner."

Christophe's eyes sparkled. "No problem. It saved me having to pack a massive diaper bag to cart to someone else's house, while inevitably forgetting some crucial item."

Everyone chuckled.

"And thank you all for coming. We haven't had a family dinner in such a long time, and with Stephen here this week, it felt like the perfect time. We're just missing Annie and Phillipe."

"We'll see you all in October at the wedding," Annie said, her voice tinny from the tablet speakers.

"Anyway, we really wanted you all here because we wanted to let you know that grandchild number three is on the way."

A chorus of congratulations rose from the table. Esme smiled, delighted that the family was so happy but feeling distinctly out of place, being included in something that was so personal.

"How're you feeling?" Charlotte asked.

Gabi shrugged. "Mostly good. A little morning

sickness hanging on, but it's rare." She flashed a quick smile. "Will waits on me hand and foot."

"As he should," decreed Aurora. "Oh, congratulations, both of you." She went forward to kiss Gabi's cheek and then Will's. "I'm delighted."

"Now Bella and Burke just need to up their game," Christophe said.

Esme smiled at the banter, loving how normal the Pembertons were despite the opulent trappings of their lives. Thankfully, no one mentioned Stephen's single status. She wondered what it would be like to carry Stephen's child. Would he be a doting father? Practical? Happy? She'd wanted children with Evan, but he'd always wanted to wait. But wasn't this getting way ahead of herself? She and Stephen weren't even in a relationship. They'd spent one night together, that was all.

Aurora also passed by and put a hand on Esme's arm. "Esme, I missed you in the kitchen, but it's good to see you again. And to see Stephen so... unclenched."

Esme choked out a laugh and Aurora treated her to a sideways smile. "I do know my children," she said, giving Esme a wink.

"I told her the same thing, Maman." Bella laughed beside her.

So much laughter. And chatter. The food was delicious, the wine perfect, and for a few blissful minutes, she found herself with a sleeping baby in her arms. It awakened all the nesting urges she'd pushed down over the years, and she swallowed against a tightening in her throat. She still wanted children, and she was already thirty-four. She cuddled the blanketed bundle close, loving the baby smell that rose from the soft cap of curls so much like Christophe's.

By eleven they'd all departed, and Stephen and Esme were back in a cab on their way home. Well, Stephen's home. Not hers.

"Tonight wasn't too much, was it?"

It had been fine. More than fine. Not a single member of his family had expressed an issue with her presence. "Everyone seemed happy you were a little more chill than normal."

"See? I told you. Ogre. I must make a point to be grouchier. I have a reputation to uphold."

She laughed.

"Do you want to go out for a nightcap? Or head to the flat?"

"To the flat, I think," she replied. "I'm actually really tired. It's been a long day, with a lot going on."

They arrived at his building and got out of the cab and into the hush of the night. Her heels clacked on the pavement but soon they were inside and going up the elevator to his floor. When they reached his door, she let out a long sigh. She was reluctant for her magical time in Paris to end. But she needed sleep, too.

"Let me help you get off your feet." He swept

her up in his arms, and she curled into his embrace.

"Stephen?"

"Hmm?" He kicked off his shoes, shut the door, and started walking toward the bedroom. Her heart fluttered. Was he taking her to her room, or his?

"Everyone keeps saying you were so grumpy before. That you didn't smile as much. And, I mean, I kind of saw that when you first came home."

He stopped in the doorway to his bedroom, then set her down. He took her hand and led her to the bed, sat, and patted the mattress beside him.

"Es," he began, "it's true. Sometimes I've been a jerk. Part of it was trying to protect the people I love from getting hurt like I was. But a lot of it came from me being unhappy and dissatisfied. It's not that you've changed me, really. It's that when I'm with you, I'm happy, so the other stuff fades away. I'm not proud of all my actions in the last two years. But you…you don't just make me happy. You make me want to do better."

"Oh," she said, trying not to cry at the sweet words.

"I know we're taking this a day at a time, and I know I'm not usually one to talk about my feelings, but I think you should know that."

She reached up and wrapped her arms around him. And as his arms tightened around her, she prayed she would be strong enough to never let him down. And yet she was so unsure about everything. Where did they go from here? Because as delightful as this forty-eight-hour interlude had been, tomorrow it was back to the real world, where he was the Earl of Chatsworth and she was plain Esme Flanagan. He didn't want love and she refused to settle. And there was only so long they could stick their heads in the sand and avoid dealing with all of it.

The return across the Channel seemed anticlimactic somehow. Stephen held Esme's bag as they made their way through customs and to the hired car, and they were both quiet on the drive from Gatwick. Reality was back with a slap. The festival was tomorrow, and Stephen only had a few days after that before he was scheduled to return to Paris. It would mean leaving Esme, just when things were developing between them. He would miss her. But then, if he really wanted to avoid an emotional entanglement, leaving was the best thing. But was that what he wanted?

He dropped her off at her flat, walking her to the door and carrying her overnight bag and the garment bag containing the emerald silk, which he'd insisted she keep. Her closed-off expression kept him from kissing her goodbye. Well, almost. He leaned in and dropped a kiss on the crest of her cheek. "I'll see you later?" he murmured.

She nodded. "Let me unpack and check on Mum. I'll come over later and…and catch up on work."

Right. Because she was the housekeeper, maid and cook, all in one. And he was lord of the manor. He wondered if she was reminding him as some sort of defense mechanism. She'd been reserved since this morning when they'd awakened in his bed.

She was likely as terrified as he was.

Back at the manor, Stephen stepped outside into the garden and took a look at the progress. It would be weeks before all the features and plants would be installed, but the shape of it was clear. It was an odd moment, two years after Cedric's death, to realize that his father was truly gone. But there was a heavy sense of finality in the pit of Stephen's stomach.

Cedric Pemberton was gone and with him, his mistakes and flaws. There was no need to carry them into the future, for they served no purpose. Stephen let out a massive sigh and rubbed his hand over his stinging eyes.

He would not let the good memories be tainted. Instead, he looked over the garden and fields beyond and let forgiveness into his heart. Who was he to blame his father for being…human? Lord knew Stephen had made his share of mistakes.

He went back inside and to the library, where he sat at the desk and pulled out the little box with the pocket watch again. He stared at it for long minutes, turning it over in his hand, the cool gold warming from his touch. For generations, the owner of the watch had sat in this very room, making decisions for the estate and for the Pemberton family. The gravity of that settled heavily on his shoulders, but it wasn't a burden, exactly. It was, he realized, the duty to simply do the right thing.

He picked up his phone and called the solicitor, giving him instructions to expedite settling the agreement the family had informally come to with regards to Anemone's inheritance. Christophe's old flat in Paris was family-owned and still vacant; it would become Anemone and Phillipe's for when they were in Paris. There was a pearl and diamond choker that was Cedric's mother's, as well as a few other mementos that would also become hers. And the money. The five children had all agreed that Anemone should have an equal share. They would each sign over a portion of their inheritance.

Family was family, and that was that.

When his call finished, he sat back in his chair and let out a satisfied breath. And when Esme arrived at the door, carrying a tray of coffee and two cups, he sat forward with a smile.

This was all because of her. She'd been the one to help him start to heal. To help him begin to open his heart again. It was a damned miracle.

And she didn't even know it. It occurred to him that it was because she'd always known his heart. And while they'd spent years apart, that heart-to-heart recognition hadn't disappeared.

He was falling in love with her and helpless to stop it. And he couldn't be bothered to try. Because this was Esme.

He trusted her.

"You're back." He got up from the desk and took the tray from her hands, noticing her cheeks turned pink. "Everything okay with your mum?"

Esme nodded. "I think so. The side effects from her last chemo are easing a bit. She's getting ready for her booth at the festival tomorrow."

He lifted his eyebrows as he put down the tray. "She is? Isn't that a lot of work?"

"Tell my mum that. She puts tarts and jam into the contest every year. Marjorie might be the cook here, but Mum can hold her own."

He shook his head. "Now I see where you get your stubbornness." But he smiled. He liked that she wasn't a pushover. Whatever her past with her ex-husband, she'd clearly moved into her own sense of independence. He looked at her closer. "Es, are we okay? You've been so quiet all day."

"Just in my head a bit." Her eyes shuttered a little, closing him out, but he wouldn't press. If she needed time to wrap her head around things, he understood. He'd been less than two weeks and in that time they'd reconnected, slept together, she'd met his family…again. Not as Mrs. Flanagan's daughter, but as his guest.

It was a lot.

"I understand." He poured coffee instead, handing her a cup fixed with a little milk and sugar, the way he'd discovered she liked.

"Things changed between us, Stephen. But I'm still the housekeeper… I think I'm just having difficulty sorting through the dynamics of everything."

"Give it time," he said quietly. "But don't shut me out, Esme. And for God's sake, don't lie to me."

Her gaze warmed a little. "I know that's a tough one for you, after Bridget and Gabi."

He nodded, his jaw tightening. "It is. I'd rather know the truth up-front, even if it isn't what I want to hear."

Esme put down her cup and went to him. "Oh, Stephen, I know that. I'm sorry. I really am in my head right now. Paris was…amazing. But it's all so new and overwhelming, and you're leaving again in a few days, and I guess I'm just trying to protect myself."

Which he also understood. And if she was overwhelmed, she definitely wasn't ready to hear the truth about his feelings.

"Let's just have a quiet dinner tonight and… maybe you can stay? But only if you want to."

She nodded, laying a cool hand on his cheek.

"I would like that. I'd like that a lot. If we only have a few more days, I don't want to waste them."

He leaned down and kissed her, a soft, reassuring kiss that still managed to fire his blood and fuel his desire. A few days…yes. But the more time he spent with her, the more he was reconsidering whether being in Paris full-time was where he wanted to be. The first day he'd come back he'd felt the pull of home. Now, with Esme here, the pull was even stronger.

CHAPTER TWELVE

Esme tucked the vacuum away and wondered if Stephen was still in the library. This afternoon he'd put her mind at ease, at least a little. But she was still going back and forth in her head about what she wanted. She hadn't lied. Paris had been amazing, but fairy tales were not day-to-day living. That was done right here, at Chatsworth and in the village. Here, she and Stephen seemed to fit together like peas in a pod. In Paris, though, she was firmly reminded of the life she'd been glad to leave behind.

She wasn't going to let those thoughts ruin the last few days they had together, though, so she stuck her head into the library and said, "How about some dinner?"

"I could eat," Stephen said. "What's in the fridge?"

"I'm not sure. Let's investigate."

What she really wanted to do was pick up where they'd left off, in his arms and tasting his sweet kisses.

Once in the kitchen, she went to the refrigerator and stuck her head in the door. "There's some chicken, some salad greens... I can work with that."

"It's fine with me," he said. "After the feast last night, I could do with something lighter."

She set him about washing greens and cutting up veg for the salad while she sauteed the chicken. She added butter, herbs and white wine, whipping up a heavenly-smelling sauce. As it simmered, she made a simple vinaigrette with olive oil and balsamic vinegar, and before long they were sitting at the table, enjoying another meal together.

Stephen took his first bite and sighed. "Esme, this is delicious."

"I've picked up some things after so many years working in the service industry," she said, pouring them each a glass of wine. "There's nothing in the world that butter and a splash of wine can't make better."

He laughed.

They finished the meal and worked together to tidy the kitchen. It felt so natural to her, so right. She imagined what it would be like living together like a normal couple, standing together doing dishes in the evening. There was a rightness to it that settled in her heart. But that was foolish, wasn't it? Here at the manor, there were usually several staff on duty, and she remembered he'd told her he had someone come into his flat in Paris to clean and take on some cooking duties.

"You okay? You've been drying that plate for five minutes." He smiled at her with affection. "Or have you disappeared into your head again?"

"Something like that," she admitted.

He took the plate from her hands, put it away and returned to her. "I have a cure for that," he said.

She couldn't stop the smile that blossomed on her lips. "Oh, do you?"

"Mmm-hmm." He slid closer and clasped his hands at the base of her spine. "I have a few ways to take your mind off troubles. Care to hear them?"

"I'd rather you show me," she admitted.

They abandoned the rest of the dishes as Stephen took her hand and led her from the kitchen, anticipation simmering in her belly. Her footsteps were muffled on the carpet runner on the stairs, halting only when he paused to open the door to his room. Maybe they needed to talk about their relationship, but right now she wanted something more.

Once they were inside, she shut the door and reached for the buttons on his shirt. He held his breath, letting her undress him, his body growing rock-hard beneath her gentle touch. He lifted his hand and touched her hair—God, how she loved the way he looked at her—and reminded herself to be patient, that they had all night.

Once his shirt was off, she reached for her own, undoing the buttons and sliding it off, then slipping out of her bra. In the next breath, she was pressed up against his chest, skin to skin, in heaven.

It blew her mind how she could be so lucky to find the perfect lover in a best friend. But when they finally reached the bed and she fell apart in his arms, she knew she never wanted to let him go. And yet she'd have to, because after thinking all day, she still couldn't see a way to be a part of his world and still be herself.

The next morning the fair opened, and with it the local exhibits from artisans, cooks, and crafters. She asked for the morning off as Mary was determined to enter her wares in the gooseberry categories just as she had for the last twenty-odd years. It meant precious hours away from Stephen, though he'd ended up holing up in the library anyway, working on something or other.

They loaded up Esme's little Renault with boxes of jam, jellies, and tarts that Mary had baked the two days before. Some would be entered for judging, with the rest going on Mary's table to be sold. In addition to the gooseberry items, there were also various chutneys, strawberry preserves, raspberry jelly, pasties, and currant tea cakes. All recipes Mary insisted she'd learned from her mum, and Esme couldn't argue with their success. Every year someone new booked a table with fancy cupcake holders and tons of buttercream-topped goodies, but they came to Mary's table for home-cooked favorites.

No wonder her mum was exhausted.

They arrived at the fairgrounds and Esme looked over at Mary. Her color was still off. "Are you sure you're up to this, Mum?"

"I haven't missed the festival in over twenty years, and I'm not going to let cancer keep me from being here this year." Her mother's voice was firm, and Esme couldn't argue. That determination was so important for her mum's recovery.

"Well, will you let me look after setting up? Why don't you have a cup of tea with the WI ladies?"

"I might do." Mary looked at Esme. "Thank you, Es. You shouldn't have to look after your old mum."

"As if." Esme snorted, tamping down the emotion that swamped her chest. "Besides, you looked after me and I was no picnic."

Mary laughed. "I should help—"

"Don't give it a thought. You wander over in about thirty minutes and I'll have it all ready for you."

Mary nodded as they got out of the car, and

with a small wave, headed in the direction of the WI tent and tea.

That concerned Esme more than anything. Her mother had capitulated too easily. It wasn't like her. Worry cascaded through her chest as she watched her mum walk away. What if the chemo wasn't working? What if the cancer came back worse than before?

She grabbed her phone and tapped out a quick text message.

Would it be all right if I took the whole day off? Worried about Mum. Going to set up for her but thought I might stay with her if possible.

The phone disappeared into her back pocket, and she grabbed the first bag of items needed for the table: her mum's "fair cloth" that was really just a cotton red-and-white-checked tablecloth, the stack of little card stock signs written up in her mum's writing with the item and ingredient list, and a little cashbox with a tiny float. She'd set up the table first and then bring up the other items.

She had just sorted the table, two chairs, and put on the tablecloth in the food items tent when a familiar figure came striding toward her, setting her pulse aflutter.

What on earth was Stephen doing here? He wasn't supposed to arrive until later this afternoon, for the judging.

"Hi," he greeted, looking rather delicious in what she supposed was his business casual dress of dark gray trousers, a fine dress shirt open at the throat and rolled to the elbows, and the Italian leather shoes he liked so much.

"Did you get my message?" she asked, unsure of what to say.

"I did. I thought I'd give you a hand. And perhaps…" He bent down and looked into her face. "Perhaps some moral support? Is Mary not doing well?"

She loved how he cared so much. "Maybe I'm worrying for nothing, but she seems so tired, and she's pale. She spent the last two days baking, and I probably should have been here to help her. When we got here I suggested she find a cup of tea and I'd set up and she didn't even argue."

Worry puckered Stephen's eyebrows, and she was relieved that it wasn't just her that was concerned about her mother's uncharacteristic behavior. "Well, let's get her set up."

She tried to ignore the warm feeling that went through her, knowing he'd dropped everything to come help this morning. Instead, she focused on loading his arms and hers with items from the car and carting them back to the table. Once there, Stephen suggested he do the rest of the lugging while she arranged the items. By the time he'd returned with the next load of jams and jellies, she had the table half-full of goodies, as well as the little sign her mum used that quaintly announced *Mrs. Flanagan's Fancies.*

They worked together, stocking the table and then stowing the extra stock beneath the skirting. When it was nearly finished, Mary came around the corner and stopped. "Oh, that looks lovely!"

She had a paper cup with steaming tea in her hand and Esme was glad to see she looked brighter than she had in the car. "It's all set up for you, Mum," she said, pulling out a chair. "You just tell me what you want taken to the contest and I'll deliver it."

Mary looked up at Stephen. "You came to help."

"Of course I did, Mrs. F." He went forward and enveloped her in a rare hug, which made Esme's eyes sting. "Though I haven't had breakfast so I would consider payment in the form of one of those pasties." He pulled back and treated her to a smile. Oh, how irresistible he was when he smiled and the hard edges of his face softened.

Her smile brightened and she tsked at him. "Of course you shall have one." She moved behind the table and made short work of putting a golden-brown pastry in a napkin and then into his hand. "There you go. Better than even Marjorie's, though she'll deny it." Mary sent him a wink.

Stephen took the obligatory bite. "Mmm. Delish, Mrs. F."

Esme watched as her mother blushed. Blushed! It was all she could do to hold back a chuckle.

"Are you all set now, Mum? I put the cash tin just to the side there, see?" Esme showed her where the little cash box was. "And I added the signs and ingredient cards."

"You're a wonder," Mary replied, settling into her chair. "Oh, it feels good to be out and doing something. I'm not made for idleness."

Esme was going to protest, but Stephen stepped forward instead. "I'm sure," he said sympathetically. "But we all need you to get well, so rest is essential. Don't push yourself too hard, now."

"I won't."

"And I'm here to help, too," Esme said.

Mary looked up in alarm. "But you have to get back to work. I'm fine here, truly."

"Don't be silly," Stephen insisted. "I can manage on my own for a day. Besides, both of you should enjoy the fair." In another hour or so the midway would open up and there would be rides, too. All the vendors would be selling their wares and the good-natured but sometimes cutthroat competitions would begin.

"Shall I take the samples over for the judging?" Esme asked.

"That would be lovely, dear. Thank you."

"I'll help," Stephen offered.

Esme went to work packing the items Mary gave her in a shallow box. Mary hesitated with the last jar, making Esme look up at her.

"Are you sure you know what you're doing, darling?"

There was no sense pretending she didn't understand. "It's okay, Mum. I promise." She kept her voice low so Stephen couldn't hear, though he'd wandered down the aisle in the tent, looking at the other tables. "We're just friends."

"I'm not sure of that. I've never seen him look at anyone like he looks at you. He cares for you. He took you to Paris."

"I care for him, too." She chanced a look over at him to be sure they wouldn't be overheard. "But our friendship is more important. And our lives are too different." She took the final jar and tucked it into the box. "Mum, I know we don't talk about Evan, but he was so critical of me. I'm certain I couldn't handle Stephen's world, living under a microscope. My eyes are open, don't worry."

"I just want you to be happy."

At that, Esme smiled. "Well, I do too!" she said. "Love you. Now sit and enjoy the sunshine while we've got it."

"You two should enjoy the fair, too. You don't have to sit with me."

"What if we take in the events and come to check on you periodically?" That came from Stephen, who'd returned from his wander and caught the last of their conversation—and hopefully nothing earlier.

"I'd enjoy that. And if you happened to find

yourself at a curry truck at lunchtime..." Mary's eyes twinkled, and Esme was happy to see it. Maybe she did just need to be out and doing something vital.

Mary took a currant cake and pressed it into Esme's hand. "You probably didn't have breakfast," she said, in a very mom-like way.

"I'm not going to eat all your profits."

"It's one cake. Go, have fun. Stephen, you probably haven't been to the fair in years."

"Not since the last time Esme and I were here, I don't think, Mrs. F. And things have changed a lot since we were kids."

"Indeed," Mary replied, packing a lot of subtext into that one word.

"All right then. Where to first, m'lord?" Esme looked up saucily and then took a bite of her tea cake.

"I think we should scout out the competition," he said, and reached down and took her hand.

Esme wasn't sure what to do. To hold his hand in public...too much of a statement. To withdraw...awkward. In the end she waited until they'd walked a half-dozen steps, then extricated her hand from his grasp, despite how nice it felt cushioned in his strong fingers.

Stephen didn't react, but she felt the difference between them. And it wasn't that he shut her out or became cold. Instead, the awareness between them ratcheted up to about a zillion. Because not touching each other did absolutely nothing to curb the fact that they wanted to.

Stephen couldn't remember when he'd last spent such a day.

The village fair had changed in some ways, but in others remained the same country fair he remembered as a child. The Women's Institute had their cakes for sale, from gorgeous, layered concoctions swirled with icing and adorned with fresh flowers to the requisite sponge and the plain but no less delicious lemon drizzle. There were still the craft tables, but they were augmented by artisans with blown glass, paintings, and jewelry. There were even workshops available for both children and adults, which Esme tried to convince him to try but he balked. At noon they bought chicken tikka at what Esme decreed the best curry truck, and took a Styrofoam container back to Mary, who was faring well at her table, chatting and selling her goods at a brisk clip. Stephen and Esme found a rare empty picnic table with an umbrella and sat to eat their lunch together.

It was so…normal. So lovely. And he hadn't thought about work or responsibility once.

Esme smiled up at him and his heart caught.

It was a strange moment to realize he wanted her in his life forever, but he supposed there was never any real rhyme or reason to it. One moment, a tantalizing bite of curried chicken, then next, wham. His heart had pretty much left his body. And it was inconvenient as hell. Esme had made it clear that she wasn't up to an actual relationship. Wasn't that just his luck? He finally, finally found the right woman, but he wasn't the right man for her.

He understood what it was like to be burdened with the weight of expectation, of worrying he was never good enough. But he would never do that to Esme. He loved her just as she was. Could he make her understand that?

The fact remained, he'd gone and fallen in love for the first time since Bridget. And it was exhilarating and scary and so darned wonderful he wasn't sure what to do with it all.

He had no idea how to bridge the gap between them. To compromise. He couldn't change what he was. He was, and always would be, the Earl of Chatsworth as well as Aurora Germain's son. He was responsible for the estate as well as a good chunk of the Aurora, Inc. empire. He could no more walk away from his responsibilities than he could grow wings and fly. But how could he ask her to leave her life behind for him? That was hardly fair.

"You got awfully serious all of a sudden," Esme observed, dabbing her lips with a paper napkin. "Are you all right?"

He smiled. "I am. I was thinking that I spent the whole morning not thinking about work, or the estate, and just focused on relaxing and it was amazing."

She smiled back. "But then you started thinking about work?"

"Exactly," he lied, because she wasn't ready for the truth about his feelings. "Let's check out the rides," he suggested. "The last time I was here, there weren't any. Just Splat the Rat and the usual games."

Esme laughed. "It's changed some. The town's grown, and for the last few years there's been a traveling funfair that sets up at the same time as our local event. It's brought in nice crowds."

Something else he'd missed in all the busyness of his life. "I'm game if you are."

"Let's check on Mum first, and then you're on."

Mary was managing fine, though Esme made sure to take her a fresh cup of tea. Stephen then led the way to the part of the fairgrounds that housed the small midway and games.

They bought a string of tickets and first headed to the Tilt-a-Whirl, sitting together on the padded seat and holding on as the car spun around in every direction, depending on the angle of the track. Esme made the car spin even faster by leaning into the curve, the sound of her laughter ringing in the air. When they were finished there, they hit The Scrambler, tame but fun, and then she got him into the bumper cars.

There was no sitting together and holding on

for this ride. Instead Stephen found himself ensconced in a purple "car" while Esme was in a green one, and a handful of others were in other cars, each person for themselves. Stephen was hesitant until one boy who couldn't have been more than seventeen rammed the side of his car, and then all bets were off. He cranked the wheel and started off, focused on retribution when he was jolted from behind—Esme had snuck up and rear-ended him.

She was still laughing. God, it brought back memories. Back in the day there hadn't been rides, but they'd run through the fair and played games and ate candy floss until they were nearly sick. She'd laughed then, too. He remembered she was always laughing. Until the day he'd said he was going away to school.

That day she'd cried.

He understood the feeling now, because the thought of going back to Paris without her made him feel horribly empty.

"Come on, Stephen! Give it to him!" Esme was cheering him on, and he shook off his thoughts and got back into the game, laughing as everyone bumped everyone else with abandon.

When it was over, she got out of her little car, grabbed his hand and pulled him over to the candy floss stand. In moments he was holding the blue-and-pink spun sugar in his hands, feeling like he was about sixteen years old, running through the fair with the girl he had a crush on.

He took a bite and winced. "My God, that's sweet."

She wrinkled her nose and took a bite of her own. "You could use some sweetening up."

If they were alone he would snag her around the waist and kiss her teasing mouth, but since they were in public, he held back. "I probably could," he admitted. "But this…wow. Good thing I'm not diabetic."

She laughed again, and they started walking among the rides and games. "So, what's next?" she asked. "We still have a few tickets left."

"The Ferris wheel," he said, lifting his chin at the ride that towered over the others. "I know it's slow, but—you're going to think this sounds silly—this village, the estate…it's my home. And at the top of the wheel, I can see so far and feel…"

She stopped and looked up at him. "Your roots."

He nodded, a little choked up that she understood him so well. More and more he was questioning the need to spend so much time in Paris. What if he were here, at Chatsworth, more often?

"You can take the earl out of the county, but you can't take the county out of the earl," she said, jostling him with her shoulder. "Which is as it should be. You should have a connection here."

The connection was more than just geography. He was coming to realize that now. He'd been sent away to school and then to Paris and it had all been to make him a better steward—of the title, the land, and even the company his parents had built. The irony struck him. He'd had to go away to truly appreciate how very tied he was to the place he'd only visited in recent years.

He thought of the Paris flat. It was luxurious, exclusive, beautiful. It had everything he could want. But it wasn't home. And he wondered if that was part of the reason why he never seemed quite settled or content, and why others saw him as…a grump. That wasn't the man he wanted to be. But he was thirty-five. Pretty sure the die had been cast.

They were at the Ferris wheel now. They each handed over their last tickets and got into the seat, waiting while the security bar was locked around them. For a few minutes, they only moved by increments, as the person running the ride stopped to let on more people.

The wheel started to move smoothly, arcing over the top and descending to the ground again. Esme had gone quiet; something had changed between their conversation about home and getting on the ride together. It wasn't even a bad quiet; more like she was waiting, though he wasn't sure for what.

They went around the bottom, starting the incline again, until they got closer to the top. Stephen looked out over the valley and felt a pang in his chest. He loved it here. He always had. He'd been a carefree boy, laughing and smiling. When had all that changed? When he'd gone off to boarding school at thirteen? In university? Taking on increasing responsibility at Aurora? He had laughed more during this visit than he'd had in years.

Esme reached over and took his hand. "It's beautiful, isn't it?"

Beyond the village were green fields, broken by lines of trees and roads. The English countryside was beautiful.

"It is. It's home."

"I'm glad you realize that."

He faced her as they made another turn around. "What does that mean?"

"It means that you've been running. Ever since you left for school, the manor house has only been a place you visit, even if you call it home." She looked out over the fairground, over the fields beyond, and let out a replete sigh. "I'm connected to this place. It's part of me, no matter where I go. But I've stayed because my heart is here. Despite all the bad things."

"Bad things," Stephen echoed, unsure of what she was getting at.

"My dad dying. The bullying when I was older. My failed marriage. Mum's cancer." She shrugged. "There are reminders of the not great things here, certainly. But there are so many good memories, too. My childhood with you. My best friend, Phoebe, whom you've yet to meet. My mum. The way it feels to go into a pub and have them know your standing order. Shopping at the market where you chat with the cashier about whatever the town is buzzing about. Walking to work and smelling the geraniums, unless it's tipping down and you're under an umbrella. Things I would miss if I left. Things I wouldn't find anywhere else."

God, she was the purest, loveliest person he'd ever met. And her description of her life wasn't perfect, and yet somehow seemed idyllic in its simplicity and beauty.

Perhaps it was time to stop running. Stop avoiding what was right in front of him and start running to the life he craved.

He put his hand along her face, leaned over, and touched his lips to hers.

Esme knew she should stop the kiss, but she was helpless to. His lips felt so good on hers, so right. At age six, he'd been her everything. Now, at age thirty-four, he was rapidly moving into that role again, and as much as it terrified her, she couldn't make herself pull away.

Instead, she kissed him back.

He was capable of such tenderness. This kiss was different from their previous ones. Less fevered, less surprising, but with a connection that ran straight to her heart. It was generous, giving. Sweet and loving. And this simple kiss on a Ferris wheel was even more devastating than what had transpired between them in Paris and last night.

Their lovemaking had been fueled by passion. This, though…this was different. She felt herself falling and lacked the will to put on the brakes. Her heart was well and truly involved now.

The wheel stopped, halting them at the top, the seat swinging slightly. Esme finally broke the kiss, then rested her forehead against his. "Stephen," she whispered.

"Don't say it," he said. "Not if you're going to say we can't be together."

She sat back a little so she could meet his gaze. His dark eyes were wide and full of emotion, so much that it frightened her a little, even while deep down she rejoiced in it. It complicated everything, but this thing between them…it was real. Not just a quick tumble, getting each other out of their systems, or even simply satisfying a need.

"I'm falling for you, Esme. I didn't plan it. I know how you feel about my life. But I have to be honest about my feelings. I've spent my whole life not being honest. I've glossed over my emotions, camouflaged them with ambition and this…façade. I'm tired of being that man. I'm not that man with you. With you… I'm who I'm meant to be."

The attendant was letting people off; they

moved another increment over the apex, toward the bottom.

"Oh, Stephen…" She thought about her life here, her safe, predictable life. She'd meant everything she'd said only minutes earlier about why she loved it and why it was home. But perhaps there was another way of running away. Perhaps she'd run away from a lot of possibilities, hiding behind her contentment.

She suddenly realized that if she walked away from Stephen now, without trying, she would always regret it.

"I'm scared," she admitted. "Scared of what it would mean to actually be with you. Not as the housekeeper's daughter. Not as an old friend… but *with* you."

"I know that. But we can take it slowly, can't we? There's no need to take out a page in the *Times* or anything."

She laughed. "You're right. Except…you're leaving soon." The knowledge washed over her, killing the flash of excitement she'd felt.

The wheel moved again, then stopped. There were only two seats left before they'd have to get off the ride. Somehow she didn't want to. She wanted to stay on here forever, where nothing could change, and it would just be the two of them.

Stephen held her hand tightly. "Maybe I can stretch things out a little longer, until we see how we feel. I know you have reservations and rightly so. But…what if we miss out on something really good? I have trust issues, Es. But I trust you. Doesn't that tell you something?"

They were nearly at the bottom now, and suddenly it seemed like a ticking clock, like something had to be decided before the wheel stopped turning and they had to get off. He was leaving it up to her. They could go in one direction, staying friends, staying safe and comfortable. Or they could take a different path, take a risk, see what happened. She thought about what life with Stephen would entail. Could she do it?

She didn't know. But just as surely, she knew she had to try. She would wonder *what if* forever if she didn't.

"I'd like you to stay," she said, looking into his eyes.

The moment the words were out of her mouth, it felt as if everything shifted. They were no longer dancing around desire and need but moving into relationship territory. It was heady and exciting, leaving a ball of nerves tangling around in her stomach that was both anticipation and trepidation. She was not a risk taker. But this…

This was Stephen. And she'd never been able to say no to him. Not really.

"Es," he whispered, just as their seat jolted to a halt at the bottom and the attendant reached for their safety latch.

They got out of the bucketed seat and went

through the exit. Esme's heart seemed to be dancing a little jig right there in her chest, but they walked away as if nothing had changed. He didn't reach for her hand—it appeared being discreet was still a thing, and for that she was glad. She wasn't ready to go public with this. It was bad enough they'd kissed on the ride.

But then to her surprise he tugged her behind a canvas tent and pulled her into his arms, planting a kiss on her startled lips. "To tide us over until later," he said, gazing into her eyes.

This was the Stephen she remembered. Game to take a chance, laugh, have fun. The Stephen that had existed before boarding schools and universities and billion-dollar industries and titles. She loved this version of the man so much, but would that disappear once he was back in his usual world? She was enough now, but would she always be?

Enough with the negative talk, she told herself sternly. They'd agreed on one day at a time, and she wasn't going to indulge in a self-fulfilling prophecy. She stood on tiptoe instead and pressed her lips to his once more, a fleeting kiss that still echoed right down to her toes.

When she lowered her heels again, she sighed. "The hardest part is going to be pretending that nothing's changed," she said softly. "With Mum, mostly."

"But only until we're sure. We need a little time to be certain this is—"

"Exactly." Esme nodded, then changed the subject. "So what now, Lord Pemberton? More of the fair, or are you done for the day?"

He smiled at her. "More. We haven't even played Splat the Rat."

She burst out laughing. "Truly? That's what you want to do?"

"It is. Should we bet on it?"

"Only if we go to the Coconut Shy after."

"Done."

Esme couldn't remember the last time she'd had this much fun at the fair. They dissolved into laughter as she missed hitting the rat—more than once—and then Stephen nailed him on his first try with a definitive smack. At the Coconut Shy, she did better, hitting one of the three coconuts with her ball and winning a ridiculous stuffed monkey key chain. Stephen excelled here, too, hitting all three coconuts and winning a foot-tall Paddington Bear, complete with hat and little boots.

He handed it to her, looking as proud as if he'd given her a diamond necklace.

They passed a few other games, but it wasn't until Esme saw the balloon pop game that she knew she was in her element. She stepped up, paid her money, and took her darts. Different colored balloons were for different sized prizes, and she took aim at the rarest color. Stephen watched quietly as she let the dart go.

Pop.

Cheers sounded from behind her, and she smiled a little, but didn't lose her focus. She took the next dart and lined up.

Pop.

More cheers, and someone called out, "Go get 'em, Esme!" She gave a little laugh, but then took her last dart and focused again. The nights spent at the local pub with pals had a purpose after all.

There were only two purple balloons left. She pulled back her arm, kept her eye on the target, and threw the dart.

Pop.

"And the lady wins the prize!" Each of the balloons held a different prize, but she had the option to put all three together and get something huge. She did—she traded in all three of her prizes for a giant brown-and-white stuffed dog, which she then handed to Stephen. It was nearly as big as he was.

She was offered congratulations when she turned around and several pairs of eyes looked at Stephen speculatively. She merely threw him a saucy grin and they started off back toward Mary's tent, wordlessly agreeing they should check on her again. After that, Stephen would go to the tent for the judging.

Esme noticed her mother seemed tired; maybe it was the heat or all the commotion, but either way she didn't want her mum to overdo it. "Mum, why don't you let me finish here? I can pack everything back in my car at the end of the day. You don't need to be here for twelve full hours."

"Oh, I couldn't ask you to do that."

"Sure you can."

Stephen came around the corner, still holding the big, goofy-looking dog. "I can take you home after the judging, Mary. It's no trouble at all. And I can come back and help Esme pack up."

Esme caught his gaze. Ah, a plan to end the day together. Clever. And then what?

"Stephen, I…" Mary shook her head, emotion etched on her face. "Your family has already done so much for me."

He gave Esme the dog and went to the table, squatting down so he could look her in the face. "Mrs. F, you're family, too. Don't you know that?"

She flapped a hand, but Esme saw the tears in her eyes. Her mum had dedicated her life to working for the Pemberton family. It was only natural she got attached to its members.

"All right," she said, giving a nod. "Esme, you know the prices."

"I do. Don't you worry about a thing."

Stephen offered to escort Mary to the competition, but before leaving he leaned toward Esme. "I'll be back," he said softly. "I won't be long."

Then the man she was falling in love with disappeared with her mother...the two people she cared for most in the world.

CHAPTER THIRTEEN

THE NEXT MORNING, Stephen dealt with the mess from their rushed breakfast while Esme headed back into the village to check on Mary. He knew she was worried her mum had overdone it the past few days, and Mary had seemed very tired last night, even though she'd been pleased as punch to take first place for her tarts and third for her jam.

He was finally ensconced in the study with a fresh cup of coffee while the landscape crew worked outside. The schedule for all the installations was planned, including the fountain and the planting of fall bulbs to ensure a bounty of color in the spring. He was due back at Aurora in a few more days. He had mixed feelings. He was ready to go back to work. But that also meant going back to Paris and leaving Esme. It was too soon. He wanted more time with her.

He was toying with the idea of working from Chatsworth for a while longer when the video call app rang. It was Bella, and he doubted this was a "catch up with my brother" call. He answered and turned up the volume. "*Bonjour*, Bella."

"Good morning, big brother." Bella's smile was warm. "How is your vacation?"

He raised an eyebrow. "I have been working, you know."

"Undoubtedly. But still finding time to take in local attractions?"

There was something in her voice that triggered some unease. "I suppose. I did go to the local fair yesterday to do the gooseberry judging." He laughed a little. "The burdens of being an earl. More gooseberry tarts than I could eat."

"Of course, I remember. You complained about it enough." Bella's easy tone slid into one a bit more guarded. "I meant more that you went on some rides. And not alone."

Cold sliced through his chest. "We were discreet."

"Apparently not. The *Mail* has a very large photo featuring the Ferris wheel, the Earl of Chatsworth, and Esme Flanagan."

Stephen dropped his head in his hands. "Can we never escape the damned press?"

"No, and more's the pity. A minor peer is one thing. COO of Aurora, Inc., however, is another story. A bigger one, apparently. Don't worry, big brother. We've all been there. Now it's your turn."

"You forget, I've already had my turn. Twice."

"Then you're a dab hand at it. Esme, however,

isn't. Are you in love with her? Is she in love with you?" Bella didn't hold back. "It looked like things were heading in that direction this week when you brought her to dinner."

His stomach rolled over. "I can only speak for myself, Bel. I'm pretty sure this is the real thing." He lifted his head out of his hands and looked his sister in the face. She was sitting in her office in Paris, looking absolutely flawless, just as she always did. "She has reservations. And this is going to play right into them." Could he not catch a break? Less than twenty-four hours ago they'd agreed to take things slowly. Now they were in the papers.

"It's not easy loving a Pemberton," Bella acknowledged. "Anyway, listen, I wanted to talk to you to see if there was even any need for damage control. The piece isn't great, but you know as well as I do that we can't respond to every story that is simply out to sell papers. I don't think any of it is *not* true. Esme is our housekeeper's daughter. And she was married before. Those are facts."

Stephen sighed. "We thought we were discreet. No one ever bothers us when we're at the house or in the village. Dammit, Bel, we talked about taking it slowly, and now this just kicks it into high gear."

"I can have Charlotte call you. Come up with a strategy."

"No, don't. I'll see if I can find the article online. As if that'll be hard." He ran his fingers through his hair. "And then I'll decide. Chances are it'll be like most every other story. We ignore it. We both know we can't try to control what the press says about us. It's like a big game of Splat the Rat. Besides, Esme is lovely just as she is. I don't give a damn if she's the housekeeper's daughter or if she's been married before."

"You know the family is behind you. Especially if this is real. You deserve to be happy too, Stephen."

Did he? Maybe not. He hadn't been the best big brother lately. Or the best earl, either. But he was trying.

"Keep me posted," Bella was saying. "And take extra time if you need to."

"No, I'll be back next week. I've been away long enough. And by the way, you'll be receiving papers soon. You all will. I think we've finally got Anemone's inheritance sorted."

"Oh, that's lovely. I know it was a difficult thing for you."

"In the end, not so much. She's as much his child as we are. And we got to have him as our father. She missed out."

"You've changed your tune."

He shrugged and met her gaze. "I'm trying this new thing called deciding what sort of earl I'd like to be. For the estate and for the family."

Bella's smile was soft and reminiscent of their

father's. "Well, that sounds grand. Now, I've got to go, but reach out if you need help with the media storm."

They clicked off the call and Stephen sat back in his chair, swiping his hand through his hair.

He'd thought they'd have time before their relationship got out. Thought maybe they'd be lucky and slip under the paparazzi radar altogether, like they had at the Paris party. But that was a naïve hope, as it turned out. And now he somehow had to get to Esme and tell her first.

Esme had ensured her mum had a good breakfast and spent an hour tidying around the flat so Mary could get a little more rest after her busy days.

"Esme, I'm fine. I promise." Still, Mary looked a bit pale. Esme wasn't convinced but recognized that might be her own worry talking. These days she was the one who felt like the parent and found it difficult not to hover.

"Mary, you won't believe what—" Judy Brown came through the door, knocking as she entered, and halted suddenly as she saw Esme. "Oh, Esme. I...well."

"I won't believe what, Judy?" Judy was Mary's neighbor and Esme had known her for years.

"Oh, well, I..."

Esme noticed she had a newspaper in her hand—she was one of the few that still read the paper copy over digital. "What's happened, Judy?"

To Esme's surprise, Judy's face turned a bright scarlet. She cleared her throat and tried a smile. "Congratulations, Esme. I didn't realize you and Stephen Pemberton were involved. What a great catch!"

Esme stilled. What was Judy talking about?

"Esme?" Mary's voice now, and Esme added guilt to the list of feelings roiling around inside her.

"It's very new," she said quietly. "We weren't really planning on going public…yet." She added *yet* because obviously they would have had to at some point. "How did you hear, Judy?"

Judy's expression softened. "It's in the paper today, love."

In the paper. Esme's body went numb. "May I see it, please?"

Judy looked like she'd been caught shoplifting—positively scandalized. "Now, Esme, you remember that reporters go for whatever will cause a sensation. It's just fluff, that's what it is."

"Clearly it's caused a sensation with you. May I see, please? Otherwise I'll just go find it online." Her voice was steadier than she might have expected, considering her insides were quaking.

"You'd better give it to her, Judy." That from Mary.

Judy handed over the paper; it was already flipped to the correct page and folded over. Esme's heart sank to her toes as the picture took up a quarter of the page, with the ridiculous headline, *Upstairs, Downstairs...*

The picture was, of course, of them kissing on the Ferris wheel.

Not a difficult photo, she supposed, considering the paps used massive zoom lenses that would surely cause them cervical spine issues later in life. That intimate moment splashed all over the paper and presumably the internet.

But the worst was the article itself. "Red-haired beauty" she supposed was all right, but it went on to highlight her as "Esme Flanagan, hotel housekeeper and divorcée" as if they were flaws, and also that her mum was the housekeeper at the manor. It painted her as a nobody—well, not a nobody, but a "healthy, country girl" which she knew was a dig at her figure. It pointed out her jeans and plain top as firmly tongue-in-cheek "high street chic," not a compliment at all. The tone beneath it all was that she was far below Stephen and how the writers couldn't blame him for tasting the "local flavors."

Oh, that last line was disgusting.

As calmly as she could, she handed the paper back to Judy. "Mum, you'll be all right for a bit, yeah?"

"Of course, darling." Mary's tone was subdued, as if she knew Esme's temper was holding on by a very thin thread.

Then Esme left the flat and walked straight

to her car. There was only one place to go—
Chatsworth Manor. And when she got there, she
had to do what she hadn't been strong enough,
smart enough to do yesterday when he'd suggested
they make their relationship into more.

She had to say goodbye to Stephen.

Stephen heard the front door slam and knew it
was Esme. He took a breath and shut the cover of
his laptop, but he already knew everything that
had been said in that horrendous article. Honestly,
didn't people get tired of being disgusting and in-
vasive?

Not that he cared. It wasn't the first time he'd
had half a page of coverage. But this was Esme's
biggest fear. By the sound of the heavy oak door,
she'd either seen or heard about it.

She appeared at the study door, hair falling out
of its pins, cheeks flushed, eyes snapping.

"You've heard," he said, keeping his voice neutral. He didn't want to make it sound like a dire
thing, but neither did he want to brush this off.
The article hadn't exactly been complimentary.

"One of Mum's neighbors had a paper this
morning. You?"

He hooked a thumb toward the laptop. "Video
chat with Bella."

Esme made a sound of disgust. "Your family
must be appalled."

"Appalled at what?"

She came further into the room. "Um, did you read it? Earl of Chatsworth *in flagrante* with the country bumpkin who changes sheets for a living."

Stephen could be a patient man, but he was also a man of strong opinions, and right now he was annoyed that the classist garbage in the paper was being repeated.

"First of all, I would hope you know my family better than that," he replied, standing in front of the desk. "When have I ever looked down on you because of your job? What about how the family welcomed you just a few nights ago? They're irritated at the press, not at you, and Bella wanted to know if we wanted any help with damage control. They, like me, do not care about what you do for a living. They care that whoever I'm with makes me happy. Full stop."

That set her back on her heels a bit, and he hoped she was taking a few moments to cool down and think things through.

"Moreover," he said, "I can't believe you just said the words *in flagrante*."

Her gaze met his, mellowed a little, and her lips curved the tiniest bit. "I might have been reading a few too many historical romances," she admitted. "But seriously…the Ferris wheel? What paper sends someone to cover a tiny village fair with a few rides and some gooseberry jam?"

Stephen sighed. "Honestly, it could have been

any local journo with a decent zoom lens, on site to cover the event. Selling that photo to a paper is pure profit. Then a few online searches and bam! You have yourself a story."

Esme began to pace. "But it was so…so…" She halted, turned to face him. "It made me sound awful."

She started pacing again.

"I know, darling, and I know it is exactly what you were afraid of. The criticism, after all the hard work you've done since your divorce. Which is not a dirty word, like they made it sound. You left and made a healthy choice for you. Look, the papers and websites are after eyeballs. The more sensational, the better."

She stopped and looked at him again. "This isn't your first experience."

"No, but it's yours, and I remember how awful it was when Gabi left me at the altar. We actually ended up in full damage control mode. This time, though, it's easy. My answer will always be that I've fallen for the loveliest woman on the planet who makes me happy."

She was at a loss for words for a few moments, but then she shook her head and tears shone in her eyes. "I don't think I can do this, Stephen. It took our one day at a time thing and obliterated it. Now not only does the village know, but also the whole country."

He took a deep breath, wanting to stay calm

rather than give in to the panic that was strangling his lungs. He didn't want to lose her, not when they were just getting started. "Es, the thing is, now that the story is out there, people are going to talk. They're going to do that whether you're with me or not. I'm so sorry this happened, and so soon, but the best thing is to ignore it. Get on with our lives. It'll blow over. It always does."

"That is easy to say when you're the hero of the story, and I'm the gold digger with a spotty romantic history and an empty bank account. When you're the handsome billionaire and I'm plain and…what was the word they used? Dowdy."

He moved toward her. "Esme Flanagan, you are not, have never been, and could never possibly be, dowdy."

"I've had those jeans for at least five years and the shirt was one from the bargain rack."

"So?" He frowned and reached out, holding her upper arms in his hands. "Why does it matter so much what one person thinks? Or even many people? We know the truth."

She pulled away and shook her head. "I can't. Today's story was me being dowdy and poor. If I stay with you, I'll be in the public eye more and more. How long before they comment on the size of my breasts or hips, the blemishes on my face, start picking apart my body?"

"You'd give away what we have, what we could

have, because of the words of a few journalists? What we have…what I feel for you…"

"You don't understand." She took a breath and faced him, her eyes stormy. "Do you know how long it took me, how many therapy sessions, just to be able to have fish and chips on a Friday night at the Lizard? Two years. How long I went before I stopped analyzing everything I put in my mouth or stepping on the scale every day? Do you know how hard I've had to work to gain the upper hand over my insecurities?"

His mouth fell open.

"How often I went home from an event and laid awake most of the night replaying conversations and wondered if I sounded stupid, or talked too much, or embarrassed myself?" Her voice rose. "I was supposed to be perfect, you see. And no one is perfect, and I know that. But having some stranger point out all my sore spots…it just takes me right back there again, Stephen. I'm not strong enough to do this. I wanted to be, but I'm… I'm not."

Desperation clawed at his lungs. "Then let me be strong for you. Please, don't give up on us because of this. I have my wounds too, Es. Ones that terrify me. But I'm willing to step out there and trust you. Can't you trust me, too?"

Her lower lip trembled just a bit and her eyes glistened. "I'm scared, Stephen. I'm scared of everything that's not in the neat little corner I've made for myself."

He understood that, perhaps more than she realized. He'd had his life laid out for him for years. There was comfort and safety in it, but at some point he had to step out on a limb and take a chance.

"Esme, I love you. Please don't walk away."

She took a step back, momentarily stunned. Then he watched as she regained her composure and lifted her chin. "You told me yesterday that I needed to be honest and up-front with you. I'm doing that. It's not fair to let this drag on. I'll... I'll only hurt you worse."

She was leaving him.

After years of closing himself off, of swearing he was done with affairs of the heart, he finally fell in love. And what did he get for it? Not a damned thing. The kicker was that one woman had wanted him for all that he had but not for himself. And the woman standing before him wanted him but wanted nothing to do with his kind of life.

He closed his eyes. The ache in his chest to stop hollowed him out, stealing his hope and joy.

"You're right," he said, his voice tight. "I did say that."

He'd also told her he loved her. But she hadn't said it back. Other than staring at him for ten seconds, she hadn't said anything about it at all.

He turned away, devastated and determined not to show it.

"I should go. I... You're leaving in a few days

anyway. I can call Lucinda and get her to come back a little early and she can look after whatever you need."

"Whatever you want," he said hollowly.

There was a pause, a quietness between them. He could tell she was still behind him, but if he looked at her he was going to lose it, and dammit, he would not fall apart again. Not like he had with Bridget.

"I'm sorry, Stephen. Desperately sorry. I thought I could do this, but when I saw that article this morning... I can't do a lifetime of this. It's better to end it now."

He took in a shaky breath. "Then go."

He felt her leave, felt her absence in the room once she was gone, and heard the front door close behind her. The house echoed, empty once more.

Then he sat down at the desk and pulled out the pocket watch from the drawer.

"Third time wasn't the charm, Dad," he whispered, turning it over in his hands. "But I promise to do this right. The estate will go on."

And maybe the promise seemed hollow at the moment, but it was all he had.

Esme couldn't face her mother until the next day. Instead Phoebe had showed up at her flat with two bottles of wine and a bag of dark chocolate truffles, and kept Esme's glass filled as she alternated between crying and resolving that she didn't need Stephen at all.

Now it was nearly noon, her head was still in the dull thud stage, and she couldn't imagine the thought of eating anything. Mary took one look at her and lifted an eyebrow.

"Would you like some tea? Or hair of the dog?" She gave a sniff. "Cabernet?"

"Pinot Noir," Esme said, wincing. "Peppermint tea, maybe?"

Mary went to put on the kettle.

"You look better today," Esme said. "You got some rest?"

"I did. Worried about you, but you're a big girl. I figured you'd sort it. You want to tell me what happened?"

Esme reached into the cupboard for a tea bag. "You were right, Mum. It was a stupid idea. We ignored all the problems and got involved anyway."

Mary was quiet for a long moment.

"Loving a man like Stephen is hard," Mary finally said. "There's just so…much. Yes, you two come from different worlds. That never really mattered before, but it's a big adjustment now. He's a public figure, therefore you will be, too. And the words will rarely be nice."

"Because nice doesn't sell papers or get website hits," Esme agreed. "Already, I'm painted as not being good enough for him."

Mary turned her head to stare at Esme, her eyes flashing. "That's codswallop."

Esme laughed, though it hurt her head. "Thank you for saying that, Mum."

"Esme, my love. This has nothing to do with whether you are good enough for Stephen or not. Of course you are."

"He said he loves me."

Another small silence, and then, "Oh. Well, that does change things, doesn't it?"

When Esme glanced over, Mary's eyes had softened.

Esme sighed. "He's so different from Evan. There's never a criticism. Never pointing out my flaws and using them against me."

"I never realized that about Evan, you know. He seemed so…lovely."

"He could be. But living with him… Mum, back then I chose the relationship I wanted rather than the one I had, if that makes sense. I didn't have one based on mutual affection and respect. It was…conditional. This isn't like that. But…" She dropped the tea bag into a mug. "But it changed how I saw myself. When I saw that article yesterday, I realized that I won't be able to withstand that sort of visibility and comment for the rest of my life. It doesn't matter if I love him. I would be unhappy, and I would make him unhappy."

Esme looked over and saw tears in her mother's eyes. "You know I had a wonderful relationship with your father. I wish we could have had so many more years together. And I've never re-married because I never met anyone who could live up to that. It's been lonely, Es. But I wouldn't trade those years with your dad for anything. If you love Stephen…don't be so quick to toss him away."

Esme's eyes filled with tears, and she swiped them away with a hand. "I thought you didn't want us involved. That it crossed the line."

"When it's love, it's different. Love just is." Mary folded Esme into a hug. "Sweetheart, if this is how Stephen makes you feel, you must at least try. You will regret it forever if you don't. And maybe it won't work, and you'll have to pick up the pieces, but pieces can always be picked up again. Second chances don't come around every day."

"Mum," she said, her voice thick with emotion. "I don't know if I'm strong enough."

"I don't want to see you get hurt, darling. But I also don't want to see you miss out on something wonderful. And Stephen's a good man. Not per-fect, but a good man."

"I need time to think."

"Of course you do." The kettle whistled and Mary poured water into two mugs, the bright scent of peppermint filling the kitchen. "Let's forget all about it for a while and make some bis-cuits."

And so Esme dealt with her heartache the same way she had nearly twenty years ago: in the kitchen with Mary, rolling out biscuit dough and humming along to the radio. And when she went home that night, she got out her sticky note pad and wrote, "I am strong." She stuck one, then two, then six, then a dozen of them on the bathroom mirror until she could stand back and see them all, her face framed in the middle.

"I am strong," she repeated.

And if she said it enough, maybe she'd believe it.

CHAPTER FOURTEEN

A WEEK HAD passed, during which Stephen had made the decision to base more of his time out of the manor house and less in Paris. Maybe he was a sucker for punishment for staying close to Esme, but he didn't want to lose all the positive progress he'd made. He was still dedicated to taking the title and making it his own. And he still saw Chatsworth Manor as his home, even though now there were memories of Esme in every corner.

He was standing at the top of the memorial garden, wishing for his father's wisdom, when Aurora, here after a quick visit to see Charlotte, appeared at his side.

"Wish he were here," she said softly.

"Me too, Maman." He sighed and put his hands in his pockets. "I wish I could talk to him. Have him help me make sense of everything."

"Oh, *mon petit*, of course. What is that saying…? 'It is lonely at the top.' You are navigating this alone and trying so hard not to show any weakness. That is a heavy burden, Stephen."

He nodded, his throat tight.

"Maman, I know it wasn't always perfect between you. There was Anemone…you knew about her, but you and Dad…you made it through. And your love was real. We all felt it growing up."

Aurora sighed. "It took a lot of work to get past what had happened. There are mistakes and then there are mistakes, if you know what I mean. But we loved each other. We made the decision to make it work, and that took a lot of talking. A lot. The only way to heal wounds is to acknowledge they exist, and then work through them. When you're doing that with another person, that means communicating."

He nodded. "I screwed things up with Esme."

"We figured."

He laughed then, and a burden lifted off his shoulders. Maman never minced words, and he loved her for it. "Being a part of the Pembertons… it's a lot to ask. The money, the fame…it comes with a trade-off. One that, for her own reasons, she doesn't feel she can take on."

Aurora turned to face him, her face wise and beautiful, and put her hand on his cheek. "I'm sorry," she said. "I remember when I first started going to functions with your father. Do you know, his mother brought someone in to give me etiquette classes so I wouldn't embarrass myself?"

"That sounds horrid."

"Maybe, but it saved my pride more than once.

Oh, your father didn't care. It was I who didn't want to look foolish and provincial. And back then there wasn't the internet and social media where things could go viral in half a second."

He considered that.

"Give her time, Stephen. Everything happened so quickly between you. In ordinary circumstances that's overwhelming. When it's our family, it's exponentially more complicated. If you love her, don't give up hope."

"I do love her," he admitted. "And the one thing I was most afraid of happened." He met his mother's wise eyes. "She left me. Like Bridget did."

"Bridget was a fool. Esme is smart. And she loves you. It was written all over her face. Patience, darling."

"Thank you, Maman."

"You deserve happiness. If it's with Esme, then you need to take the first step. And the whole family is behind you. Don't forget that, either."

"I love you, Maman. Dad was a lucky, lucky man."

"Yes," she said, "he was." She looped her arm through his. "Now, show me around the garden and tell me about all your plans."

The next Friday, Stephen found Esme at the pub, having her weekly night out with Phoebe. Phoebe noticed him first, and she reached over and tapped Esme on the arm.

Esme looked up. Their eyes met, and the jolt ran straight from his heart to the soles of his feet. God, she was beautiful. Her bright hair was pulled up in a messy bun, a halo of fire that he wanted to sink his fingers into. And her face…those moss-green eyes widened and then flickered with what he hoped was longing. He certainly felt that way.

"Esme," he said as he reached the table. He dragged his gaze away from her and looked down at her friend. "And you must be Phoebe."

"I am," Phoebe replied. "And I'm also finished. You can have my seat, Stephen."

"No, you don't have to—" Esme said, reaching for Phoebe.

"You two need to talk," Phoebe said, picking up her handbag. But she skirted around Stephen and went to Esme, giving her a kiss on the cheek. "Call me later," she said.

And then she was gone, leaving the two of them alone.

"May I?" Stephen asked, motioning toward the empty chair.

Esme nodded.

The waitress came by and took Phoebe and Esme's plates, and Stephen ordered a Pimm's out of more of a courtesy than a need for a drink. When she left again, Stephen met Esme's gaze, and the first thing he said was, "I'm sorry, Esme."

Her throat bobbed as she swallowed. "What

for?" she asked. "I'm the one who walked out on you."

Business was steady but not so loud that they couldn't have a conversation, though perhaps somewhere more private would have been better. His Pimm's arrived and he took a sip, but then put it down again. "For the article. For not being patient. For…well, that you had to go through any of that stuff at all."

"I reacted badly too, instead of sitting on my feelings for a bit. I got so mad, and then so scared. I couldn't see any other option."

Did that mean she wasn't quite as certain as she'd been that morning?

"I've been a wreck since you left," he admitted, holding her gaze, his heart pounding as he made himself utterly vulnerable to her for a second time. But the difference was he still trusted her. Esme was always straight with him. "You walking out poked me right in my sore spot. But Es, when we were together, I felt more alive, more myself, than I have in… I don't know how long. It was like someone came in and turned on a light, making everything bright and clear. That's something I didn't think was possible."

Esme reached for her water glass and took a drink, then put it back down, as if buying time to find the right words. "I honestly thought the part of me that wanted love and romance had dried up and died." She gave a little laugh. "Clearly it hadn't. You made me feel beautiful, and desired, and accepted."

"Because you are all of those things. And anyone who doesn't think so isn't someone who matters." He reached over and took her hand that rested on the table. She twined her fingers with his, a tentative link. "Can we talk now? Do you want to go somewhere more private?"

She nodded, and he quickly turned and caught the eye of the waitress, motioning for the check. "I'll look after this," he said. "Then we can go wherever you like."

Esme gave a quick nod and gathered her purse, but he noticed her hands were shaking. He told himself not to get his hopes up, but as she turned her green eyes up to look at him, he couldn't help himself.

Esme had simply planned on a chill supper with Phoebe. She hadn't even known Stephen was back in town. But when he walked in, all her senses kicked into overdrive. Nothing had changed for her. Nothing. They needed to talk, but all she wanted to do was step into the strength of his embrace and forget it all ever happened.

He put his hand at her elbow, a purely solicitous move, but tingles ran up her arm at the casual touch. She had to face facts: she was far from being over Stephen Pemberton.

They left the pub and walked to a nearby park.

where there was a little more privacy. A bench sat beneath a canopy of oaks, the late-day sun filtering through the leaves. "Shall we?" Stephen asked, and she nodded.

They sat. Esme turned toward Stephen, tucking her left leg under her right so she could face him. She reached out and took his hand—presumptuous, maybe, but she didn't want to go longer without touching him.

"When did you get back?" she asked.

He smiled. "I never left. Lucinda has been running the house. She's not you, though. Anyway, what you said was true. This is my home. Not just because I'm the earl but because it's in my heart. I'm changing things to spend more time here. I'll split things a little more evenly between here and Paris. It's an easy trip anyway."

He hadn't run off to Paris. He'd been here the whole time.

"That day at the fair," she began, her voice trembling just a little, "I could see my life changing, and I knew that our time together was coming to a close. I was already thinking about how we were going to try to make things work, living in two different countries most of the time. But when you said we could take it day by day, it seemed perfect."

"Until the paper."

She nodded. "Until then. And I'll be honest,

Stephen, the thought of facing that kind of scrutiny still fills me with anxiety."

"There's an important difference, though," he said softly. "Evan was the person who should have cherished you and loved you unconditionally. He was the person who mattered, and he didn't value you. But Es, you have to realize that I'd be right there beside you. You don't have to prove anything to me or be anyone other than the wonderful woman you already are. The tabloids, the gossip rags…those people don't matter, and they don't know you. I do. I, and the entire family, would be right there with you."

She hadn't considered that before. She thought of Bella and her horrible scars from her accident. How Jacob had gone from being a private security guard to being Charlotte's husband. Surely he'd had some insecure moments as someone who hadn't grown up in the same world as the Pembertons.

But thinking about both couples during the family dinner made her think that perhaps the love Burke had for Bella, and Charlotte had for Jacob, had helped deal with their vulnerabilities while in the public eye.

Because the Pembertons knew how to do one thing brilliantly: support each other.

Her heart was hammering now. Did they actually still stand a chance? It seemed they might, because here they were, talking and listening. Really listening.

"I let fear take over." She lifted her gaze to his again, found herself lost in the dark depths. This was the man who'd kissed her in the fort, changing their relationship. Who had touched her with hands like fire in moments of passion, then worshiped her with gentleness. Who had cared for her mother and told her she was family. He was the man who made her laugh and made her heart sing again. "I wasn't strong enough."

"And I didn't fight for you," he replied. "You needed to be able to count on me, and instead I let you walk away because of my own hurt pride."

"We're both a hot mess," she admitted. But she smiled at him anyway. *I am strong,* she reminded herself. And he was here again. Maybe it wasn't really over...

"I was scared of being hurt, but do you know what scares me the most now?"

She could barely breathe. "What?"

"Thinking I might have lost you forever. Going through the rest of my life without you. I can't promise I won't make mistakes." He lowered his gaze and shook his head. "I've been trying to be perfect for too long." He lifted his head again. "But if you want to work this out, I'm in. I'm a hundred percent in, because I love you. I think I always have. I know I always will."

A tear slid from the corner of her eye and down

her cheek, and she dashed it away. She wasn't a weeper! But what he'd said just now was so honest and true she couldn't help it. "I could say the exact same thing. You're not Evan. I knew that, but I used what happened as an excuse because everything was too perfect and it scared the hell out of me. But life is dreary without you in it now. I think...if you really mean it... I think I'd like to try. Because Stephen? I love you too. So much."

He closed his eyes for a moment, as if absorbing the words. "I mean it," he said, opening his eyes, and then leaned forward to kiss her.

His lips were soft and beguiling, familiar and yet new, because this was a new beginning. For once, she didn't care that they were in a public park, didn't care that someone might snap a picture and sell it to a paper or post it online. She loved him. And he loved her. Shutting out the critics would be a work in progress, but she would not let her hang-ups make her miss out on happiness. She was stronger than that. And when she wasn't, she'd learn to rely on the people who loved her.

"So we're going to do this?" he asked, pulling away a bit.

She nodded. "We are. And it won't always be easy. I think it happened so fast, and seemed so perfect, that when we hit a bump we both panicked. Let's not do that this time. Let's turn toward each other when we're scared, all right?"

"God, I love you, Esme," he said, pulling her

into his embrace. "And I've been thinking. I can certainly change the balance of my time between Paris and here. I've already started. Charlotte does it, after all. That way you're close to your mum."

"And I don't have to work at the inn. I can find something else. But I do want something, Stephen. I'm not built to be arm candy."

He laughed then, a soft, full, happy laugh. "You can do whatever you like. I know you. No one is going to stop you from getting what you want."

She looked at him for a long moment, considering his words. If she really wanted to embrace her future and leave her past behind, with all the criticism and gaslighting, there was one thing she could do to really reach out and grasp what her heart desired.

"In that case, Stephen…" She clung to his hand, her stomach trembling but her heart beating steady and strong. "Do you think you might marry me?"

CHAPTER FIFTEEN

THE WEDDING OF Stephen Pemberton, Earl of Chatsworth, and Esme Flanagan promised to be the event of the year. At least that was what the magazines and papers said as they scrambled to unearth details of the upcoming private nuptials.

The entire family had descended upon Chatsworth Manor for the November occasion. Mrs. Flanagan, recovered from her final two chemo treatments, was back part-time, helping Lucinda and the rest of the staff manage the house. Despite her daughter marrying the earl, she'd declared that being at Chatsworth Manor was where she belonged, and that's where she intended to stay. To Mary's relief, Stephen had agreed, though he'd told her that the moment she wanted to retire, she would have a house and be provided for. Esme had been delighted. And she rather suspected that retirement would come sooner rather than later, once she and Stephen started their family.

Which she hoped would be soon. But not too

soon. They were still adjusting—and enjoying—their time alone.

As alone as one could be in a big family that all worked together. Except for her. Stephen had already gifted her with an early, perfect wedding present—the deed to a boutique hotel in Paris. Her dream of running her own inn was coming true. As soon as the honeymoon was over, she would install a new manager who would run things when she and Stephen were here at the estate.

The morning of the wedding she woke in a different bed—not Stephen's. They'd both agreed to sleep separately the night before the ceremony, not that she'd slept all that well. She was too nervous, too excited. Her dress hung in the wardrobe, her shoes, too…and in an hour the house would be a hive of activity as everyone got ready. The family section of the chapel would be fairly empty, because she and Stephen had agreed to having his brothers and sisters as bridesmaids and groomsmen, though Gabi, being nearly seven months pregnant, had suggested she sit with Aurora. Esme had asked Phoebe to be her maid of honor, and Will was Stephen's best man.

A knock came on the door. "Come in," she called, and to her surprise it was her mum, bringing her a breakfast tray.

"Hello, sweetheart," she said, smiling. "I couldn't resist. You'll find it hard to eat later, so I wanted you to have a good breakfast."

"Thanks, Mum. Sit with me?"

"Of course."

There was coffee and toast and beautifully scrambled eggs, just the way she liked, as well as a bowl of fresh strawberries. "I feel so spoiled."

"After today you're going to be Lady Pemberton. A countess. I think you might have to get used to it."

Esme laughed. "I don't think so. It's not really who I am, title or not."

"Do you have what you need? I think your hairdresser is due to arrive at nine."

"I'm going to take a nice lavender bath. Try to relax."

After breakfast Mary left, and after a luxurious soak, Esme dressed in her undergarments and a silk robe. Phoebe arrived, followed by the hairdresser team—there were eight women requiring styling—and the makeup team, all from Aurora Paris. By noon, Esme was buffed and polished, dressed in an Aurora original gown—a gorgeous concoction with long, lace sleeves, appliques, and a cathedral-length veil that had made her sigh. She was about to become a countess, but she felt like a princess.

Phoebe was next to her, dressed in Esme's favorite emerald green. The bridesmaids' dresses were a clean and simple cut of the finest silk and rustled a little as Phoebe came to her with her bouquet, a stunning arrangement of white and cream flowers.

"You look… Oh, Es." Phoebe's eyes filled with tears. "Like a miracle. I'm so happy for you."

"I'm happy you're with me today." She looked around the suite. It was full of the women of her new family: Bella, Gabi, Sophie, Charlotte, Anemone, even Aurora, who'd stopped by with champagne once the clock ticked over twelve. There was chatter and laughter. Mary was there, too, sipping from a glass of champagne, talking to Aurora—for this one day she'd agreed to be a mother of the bride and not a housekeeper. Bella had insisted on taking Mary on a trip to find the perfect dress. Now her mum was dressed in a stunning navy gown, with a new wig framing her face until her hair came back in.

She was happy they all were there. And laughed when she caught Gabi's eye and the woman sent her a thumbs-up.

It seemed like no time at all that they were scheduled to leave for the chapel, and even though it was a short walk within the estate, they had cars lined up waiting as the weather had been showery all morning. She took a breath, clutched her bouquet, asked Phoebe for the tenth time if she had Stephen's wedding ring, then descended the stairs to begin the trip to the altar.

Stephen stood at the front of the chapel, his knee locking and unlocking. None of the usual platitudes eased his nerves. The last time he'd been in the family chapel, he'd been left at the altar. It was hard to forget that day, but he knew that Esme was entirely different. They were in love. God, so in love he didn't know what to do with it all. And soon...in a few moments...she'd be walking down the aisle to him, and they would take their vows.

Will stood beside him and leaned over with advice. "Don't pass out. Maman has just been ushered in."

Stephen looked over his shoulder at Aurora, who smiled at him. Then he caught a glimpse of Christophe escorting Mary to her seat and he knew it was time. The ushers joined Stephen and Will at the front of the chapel and the vicar stepped forward.

The music changed.

Behind him, Anemone, Sophie, Charlotte and Bella made their way to the front, and he saw Phoebe take her place to his left. She smiled up at him, and he smiled back—he quite liked Phoebe. And then the music changed again, and there was an audible gasp from the guests. His pulse hammered as he imagined her stepping to the door...

"Oh, my God." That was Will's voice, and it was full of awe. "Stephen, she's gorgeous."

Stephen turned around and there she was. A vision in white lace, her veil trailing behind her, her fiery curls shining beneath the sheer fabric. His throat tightened as he realized she was wearing Maman's wedding diamonds.

She was perfect. And she was walking toward him just this minute, a soft smile on her face, her green eyes alight with happiness and hope.

His miracle.

For the briefest moment, he was transported back nearly thirty years, waiting for her at the fort, happy when he saw her skipping along the path to meet him. They had come so far. Even then, she'd been the sunshine in his day. Now he'd have her for all of his days.

And as she reached the altar and he took her hand, he knew that his heart had finally come home.

* * * * *

*If you enjoyed this story,
check out these other great reads from
Donna Alward's Heirs to an Empire series*

A Proposal in Provence
Mistletoe Kiss with the Millionaire
Wedding Reunion with the Best Man
The Heiress's Pregnancy Surprise
Scandal and the Runaway Bride

All available now!